Texas Assessment Review and Practice Workbook

World Geography
EOC Assessment

HOLT McDOUGAL

HOUGHTON MIFFLIN HARCOURT

PHOTO CREDITS

Printed in the U.S.A.

ISBN: 978-054-798-9945

18 19 20   0928   19

4500757100   B C D E F G

Table of Contents

To the Student

In the spring of 2012, the state of Texas began to phase out the Texas Assessment of Knowledge and Skills (TAKS) test and phase in the State of Texas Assessments of Academic Readiness (STAAR) test. STAAR is designed to test your readiness for high school. The **Holt McDougal *Texas Test Prep Kit*** will prepare you for the STAAR test and help you pass it.

From TAKS to STAAR

The switch from TAKS to STAAR is being done to help you and all Texas students be successful as you continue your education. The switch also will help you be more competitive with other students, both nationally and internationally, when you enter into a career. AAt the high school level, the grade-specific TAKS tests will be replaced with twelve end-of-course STAAR tests, including the test for World Geography administered in Grade 9.

The chart below shows how STAAR will replace TAKS over several years, from 2012–2015.

	2011–2012	2012–2013	2013–2014	2014–2015
Grades 3–8	STAAR	STAAR	STAAR	STAAR
Grade 9	STAAR	STAAR	STAAR	STAAR
Grade 10	TAKS	STAAR	STAAR	STAAR
Grade 11	TAKS	TAKS	STAAR	STAAR
Grade 12	TAKS	TAKS	TAKS	STAAR

How STAAR Differs from TAKS

Here are the major ways in which STAAR differs from TAKS for the Grade 9 World Geography test:

• Test items are more rigorous. They "dig deeper" into what you know, or should know. Sometimes this means the questions are more difficult than before. The questions test fewer skills but test them more completely.

• The total number of test items has increased.

• Process skills are tested in the same questions that test the content standards. For example, a question might ask you to interpret a graph (process) as well as the information on that graph (content).

• The test is weighted in favor of "readiness standards." These standards are "the Texas Essential Knowledge and Skills (TEKS) student expectations that are not only essential for success in the current grade or course but also important for preparedness in the next grade or course." The supporting standards address content specific to the course.

• The STAAR test consists of 68 questions covering the four reporting categories: Category 1 History, Government, and Citizenship; Category 2 Geography; Category 3 Culture; and Category 4 Economics, Science, Technology, and Society. Of those 68 questions, 14 cover standards in Category 1, with an emphasis on readiness standards. Category 2 is addressed by 26 questions, and Categories 3 and 4 have 14 questions for each. In each of these cases, the focus is on readiness standards.

• The test will assess only the TEKS for World Geography, not for multiple courses.

• The test has a four-hour time limit.

• Your score on the test will count 15 percent towards your final grade for World Geography.

v

Holt McDougal *Texas Test Prep Kit*

The **Holt McDougal** *Texas Test Prep Kit* includes three components that prepare you to take and pass the STAAR test. These components are the Test Prep Support Book, ExamView Test Items, and Texas Test Prep Flashcards.

1. The **Test Prep Support Book** includes two main sections:

   • The TEKS Test Prep Support lists the full text of each Grade 9 TEKS standard. These are the standards that the STAAR questions cover. If you understand the TEKS, you can better understand what the questions that cover it are asking. So each TEKS is followed by a section called *What does it mean?* This paragraph clearly explains the meaning of the TEKS student expectation. Then two practice test questions help you see how that expectation, or standard, is covered in the questions. The answers are underlined. These questions aren't supposed to test your knowledge. They just give you an idea of the kinds of questions that might be asked on the STAAR test to cover that standard. They also get you comfortable with the format of the STAAR test.

   • Two full-length Texas Practice Tests help you become more comfortable with the STAAR format and with taking the actual test. These Practice Tests are set up like the STAAR test. These exact questions will not be on the STAAR test, but they cover the same topics and skills.

2. An **ExamView Test Bank** provides all of the Test Prep Support questions and the Practice Test questions in an editable format. If certain topics or TEKS are giving you trouble, your teacher can create a practice test that includes test items for those topics or TEKS.

3. The **Texas Test Prep Flashcards** consist of a set of 26 cards for World Geography. The Flashcards are in a PowerPoint format. Each card includes a question on one side and the answer on the other side. The questions cover the major content areas in World Geography that will be covered by the STAAR test. Using the flashcards can be a fun way for your teacher to quiz you.

Using all three components of the **Holt McDougal** *Texas Test Prep Kit* helps prepare you for the STAAR test and for the future.

Grade 9 World Geography
TEKS Test Prep Support

Notes

TEKS Test Prep Support

TEKS 1A

Analyze the effects of physical and human geographic patterns and processes on the past and describe their impact on the present, including significant physical features and environmental conditions that influenced migration patterns and shaped the distribution of culture groups today.

What does it mean?

This readiness standard focuses on analyzing how geography influenced events in the past and helped to shape the present. For example, physical features such as rivers and mountains can influence where people settle. As you study geographic patterns and processes, think about how these elements affected migration patterns and the distribution of culture groups.

Practice Test Items

1

LAND ROUTES OF EARLY PEOPLE

Which statement is supported by the map?

A Early North Americans were heavily influenced by South American cultures that migrated north.

B North America was not settled until glaciers began to retreat during the last ice age.

C The first settlers of South America likely arrived overseas from Europe.

D <u>Cold temperatures contributed to the settlement of the Americas.</u>

TEKS 1A, TEKS 21C

2 Pakistan broke away from India in 1947, just as India achieved independence. This division has its roots in —

A the spread of Buddhism throughout Asia

B the assassination of Prime Minister Indira Gandhi

C <u>the establishment of the Mughal Empire in the early 1500s</u>

D conflicts between the British East India Company and other European traders

TEKS 1A

3

TEKS Test Prep Support

TEKS 1B

Trace the spatial diffusion of phenomena such as the Columbian Exchange or the diffusion of American popular culture and describe the effects on regions of contact.

What does it mean?

This readiness standard considers how phenomena are spread from place to place, and how this diffusion ultimately affects different regions. The Columbian Exchange, for example, involved the diffusion of living things and culture between the New World and the Old World. Tracing this diffusion helps you to better understand how cultures change through contact with one another.

Practice Test Items

3 The Columbian Exchange resulted in a decrease in the population of Native Americans due to the introduction of —

A <u>disease</u>

B invasive species

C tobacco

D weapons

TEKS 1B, TEKS 22C

4

Caribbean Colonies		
Country	**Colony**	**Major Cultural Influences**
Spain	Cuba, Dominican Republic, Puerto Rico	Spanish language, Catholic religion
France	Haiti, Guadeloupe, Martinique	French language, Catholic religion
Great Britain	Jamaica, Barbados, St. Lucia, St. Vincent, Grenada, Trinidad and Tobago, British Virgin Islands	English language, Protestant and Catholic religion
Netherlands	Netherlands Antilles	Dutch language, Protestant religion
Denmark	Danish West Indies	Danish language, Protestant religion

What can you infer from this table?

A Catholics spoke the same language.

B Great Britain was not a major colonial power.

C <u>Protestantism was the dominant religion of northern Europe.</u>

D The Caribbean did not have language or religion until it was colonized by Europe.

TEKS 1B, TEKS 21A

TEKS Test Prep Support

TEKS 2A

Describe the human and physical characteristics of the same regions at different periods of time to evaluate relationships between past events and current conditions.

What does it mean?
This readiness standard focuses on how regions change over time and the effect of these changes. As you study a particular region, compare and contrast its human and physical characteristics at different periods in its history. Think about how important events in the past may have influenced the region's current conditions.

Practice Test Items

5

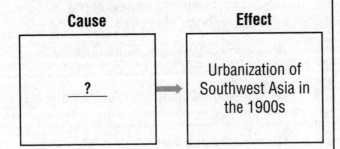

Cause	Effect
?	Urbanization of Southwest Asia in the 1900s

What cause should be placed in the flow chart to explain why Southwest Asia became highly urbanized in the 1900s?

A Search for religious freedom

B Discovery of huge oil deposits

C Immigration of political refugees

D Reduced need for farm laborers

TEKS 2A

6 For centuries, China was isolated and not a major economic force. Today, China has one of the fastest growing economies in the world because —

A much of China is rural, and most people work on farms

B the central government now plans all economic activities

C the marketplace and the consumer play a greater role in the economy

D trade restrictions have been tightened between China and other countries

TEKS 2A

GO ON

5

TEKS Test Prep Support

TEKS 2B

Explain how changes in societies have led to diverse uses of physical features.

What does it mean?
This supporting standard analyzes how change can affect the way a culture uses its resources. For example, wood was once the main fuel of early cultures. Later cultures turned to fossil fuels to provide energy. As you think about changes in resource use, ask yourself questions such as, "What prompted this change?"

Practice Test Items

7

One of the main economic activities in East Africa is tourism. The region's vast wildlife parks in Kenya, Uganda, and Tanzania are world famous. In 1938, Europeans created the game reserves because they were killing animals for sport at a high rate. Today, the parks have become important sources of income for Africans, generating millions of dollars each year from tourists.

Which is the best argument for reducing the sizes of these wildlife reserves?

A to eliminate colonial influence

B to decrease wildlife populations

C to expand urban and suburban areas

D <u>to create more farmland for growing populations</u>

TEKS 2B, TEKS 23B

8 Rain forests in Latin America are cut down to provide timber and cropland. Concerns about global warming have sparked creative ways to preserve rain forests, including —

A <u>paying off the debt of countries with rain forests</u>

B planting rain forests in regions that are not tropical

C encouraging the migration of farmers to urban areas

D imposing trade sanctions on Latin American countries

TEKS 2B

TEKS Test Prep Support

TEKS 3A

Explain weather conditions and climate in relation to annual changes in Earth-Sun relationships.

What does it mean?

This supporting standard focuses on how the relative positions of Earth and the Sun affect weather and climate. For example, the tilt of the Earth's axis as it orbits the Sun causes seasons, or short-term changes in climate. You may find it helpful to visualize the relative positions of Earth and the Sun as you study their effects on weather and climate.

Practice Test Items

9 Why do most areas near the equator have warm climates?

   A <u>They receive the most direct rays from the Sun.</u>

   C The Sun is directly over the equator at noon year-round.

   B Their surfaces reflect the greatest amount of sunlight.

   D They receive equal amounts of daylight hours and nighttime hours.

TEKS 3A

10

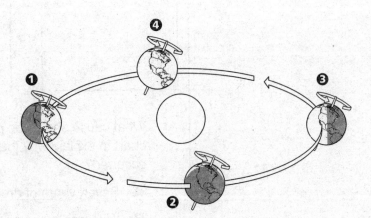

What type of weather would you expect in the northern United States when the Earth is at Point 3 in relation to the Sun?

   A <u>cold</u>

   C warm

   B moderate

   D wet

TEKS 3A

7

TEKS Test Prep Support

TEKS 3B

Describe the physical processes that affect the environments of regions, including weather, tectonic forces, erosion, and soil-building processes.

What does it mean?

This readiness standard deals with physical processes that change Earth's surface. For example, the movement of tectonic plates can result in earthquakes and volcanoes that can drastically alter the environment of affected regions. To master this standard, consider how and why these physical processes occur.

Practice Test Items

11 Which factor best explains why Japan has established a strict building code?

A It is located on the Ring of Fire.

B It is experiencing increased urbanization.

C It borders an area known as "Tornado Alley."

D It has high rates of erosion due to seasonal floods.

TEKS 3B

12   **The Dust Bowl**

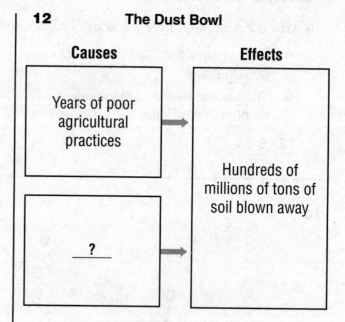

What cause should be placed in the flow chart to explain why the Dust Bowl occurred?

A Seven years of drought

B Withered crops and dead livestock

C Large migration of people to California

D Abandonment of farms in the Great Plains

TEKS 3B

GO ON

TEKS Test Prep Support

TEKS 3C

Examine the physical processes that affect the lithosphere, atmosphere, hydrosphere, and biosphere.

What does it mean?
This supporting standard focuses on how physical processes affect different parts of Earth. For example, a landslide can reshape a hillside and damage plants, animals, and people. To master this standard, you must be able to define physical processes, such as weathering and erosion, before you can examine their effects.

Practice Test Items

13 In 2004, a tsunami killed an estimated 225,000 people in Southeast Asia, South Asia, and East Africa. Which statement best describes a tsunami?

A <u>It is a giant wave associated with an underwater earthquake.</u>

B It is a powerful storm that originates over warm, tropical waters.

C It is a violent eruption caused by the movement of tectonic plates.

D It is a period of below-normal rainfall caused by stalled weather systems.

TEKS 3C

14 Plant roots can grow into crevices in rock and eventually break the rock apart. This is an example of —

A the lithosphere affecting the atmosphere through erosion

B the hydrosphere affecting the biosphere through tectonic activity

C <u>the biosphere affecting the lithosphere through mechanical weathering</u>

D the atmosphere affecting the hydrosphere through chemical weathering

TEKS 3C, TEKS 22C

9

© Houghton Mifflin Harcourt Publishing Company

TEKS Test Prep Support

TEKS 4A

Explain how elevation, latitude, wind systems, ocean currents, position on a continent, and mountain barriers influence temperature, precipitation, and distribution of climate regions.

What does it mean?

This readiness standard examines the factors that influence climate. Areas at higher elevations, for example, usually have cooler climates than areas at lower elevations. As you read about different climate regions, keep in mind which factors have the biggest influence on the climates of those regions.

Practice Test Items

15

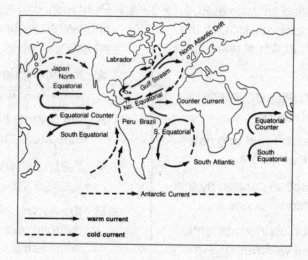

Which area on the map is most likely to have a dry climate?

A western South America

C northern Europe

B eastern Australia

D western Asia

TEKS 4A, TEKS 21C

---

16 The United States and Canada share a continent. Which factor best explains why these neighboring countries have different climates?

A elevation

C prevailing winds

B latitude

D proximity to large bodies of water

TEKS 4A

TEKS Test Prep Support

TEKS 4B

Describe different landforms and the physical processes that cause their development.

What does it mean?
This supporting standard deals with the formation of different features on Earth, such as mountains, plains, and plateaus. To master this standard, you must understand the cause-and-effect relationship between physical processes, such as uplifting, and the formation of landforms, such as mountains.

Practice Test Items

17

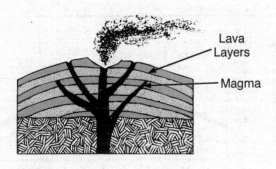

Lava
Layers

Magma

What can you conclude about this volcano?

A It formed over a hot spot.

B It is characterized by violent eruptions.

C It formed long ago and is currently dormant.

D It is composed of layers formed during gentle eruptions.

TEKS 4B

---

18 Sediments deposited at the mouth of a river form a —

A deep bay

B narrow strait

C tall, flat butte

D fan-shaped delta

TEKS 4B

GO ON

TEKS Test Prep Support

TEKS 4C

Explain the influence of climate on the distribution of biomes in different regions.

What does it mean?
This supporting standard focuses on how climate factors help determine the locations of different biomes. For example, polar biomes are found in areas with low rates of precipitation and low temperatures. As you study different biomes, look for patterns based on climate data.

Practice Test Items

19

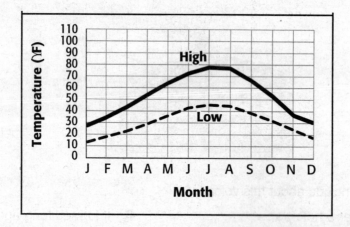

According to the temperature data in the climograph, this region would most likely be classified as —

A a coniferous forest

C a savanna

B an icecap

D tundra

TEKS 4C, TEKS 21A

---

20 A biome is classified as a savanna. It is composed of flat, grassy, mostly treeless plains. Its climate is therefore —

A maritime

C temperate

B polar

D tropical

TEKS 4C

TEKS Test Prep Support

TEKS 5A

Analyze how the character of a place is related to its political, economic, social, and cultural elements.

What does it mean?
This readiness standard focuses on how various elements shape cultural patterns and characteristics in different places. For example, religion strongly influences the political and social climate of certain countries in the Middle East. As you study different regions, analyze how political, economic, social, and cultural elements shape the regions.

Practice Test Items

21 Russians tend to cherish the countryside, as evidenced by the fact that —

   A most Russians live in rural areas

   B kasha is one of the nation's most popular foods

   C many Russians visit *banyas* at least once a week

   D <u>some 30 percent of the population owns a *dacha*</u>

TEKS 5A

22 Which of the following is an example of the long tradition of concern for equal rights that is characteristic of New Zealanders?

   A Native people in New Zealand have low rates of poverty.

   B The Maori in New Zealand obtain high levels of education.

   C <u>New Zealand was the first country to grant women the vote.</u>

   D New Zealand was colonized by countries that did not practice slavery.

TEKS 5A

TEKS Test Prep Support

TEKS 5B

Interpret political, economic, social, and demographic indicators (gross domestic product per capita, life expectancy, literacy, and infant mortality) to determine the level of development and standard of living in nations using the terms Human Development Index, less developed, newly industrialized, and more developed.

What does it mean?

This supporting standard focuses on the standard of living and the level of development of countries in various stages of development. It asks you to interpret factors, such as life expectancy, literacy rates, and infant mortality rates. You also must be able to understand terms such as *Human Development Index, less developed, newly industrialized,* and *more developed.*

Practice Test Items

23

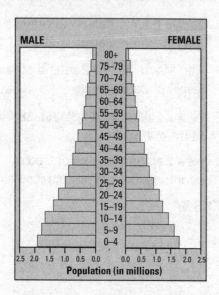

A population pyramid with this structure is usually associated with a —

A less developed nation that has a low standard of living

B more developed nation that has a low standard of living

C more developed nation that has a high standard of living

D newly industrialized nation that has a moderate standard of living

TEKS 5B, TEKS 22C

24 Which set of factors most likely corresponds to a country that is classified as more developed?

A literacy rate = low; life expectancy = high

B literacy rate = high; infant mortality = high

C life expectancy = high; infant mortality = low

D life expectancy = low; infant mortality = high

TEKS 5B, TEKS 22C

14

TEKS Test Prep Support

TEKS 6A

Locate and describe human and physical features that influence the size and distribution of settlements.

What does it mean?
This supporting standard focuses on the elements that affect human settlements in terms of size and distribution. To master this standard, you should consider both human and physical elements. A high immigration rate, for example, is a human element that contributes to the size of settlements. Proximity to a large body of water is a physical element that contributes to the distribution of settlements.

Practice Test Items

25 Why did the population of Rwanda shrink by about one million in the mid-1990s?

   A Disease and lack of medical care decimated the population.

   B <u>People moved to other parts of Africa, following a civil war.</u>

   C The government waged a successful campaign to reduce birthrates.

   D A severe drought led to the deaths of hundreds of thousands of people.

TEKS 6A

26 An estimated 25 million Europeans died during the 1300s as a result of the bubonic plague. Which of the following could hypothetically have slowed the spread of the disease?

   A an increase in temperature

   B improved access to clean water

   C a reduction in the mosquito population

   D <u>a temporary halt in trade between East and West</u>

TEKS 6A

TEKS Test Prep Support

TEKS 6B

Explain the processes that have caused changes in settlement patterns, including urbanization, transportation, access to and availability of resources, and economic activities.

What does it mean?
This readiness standard analyzes why settlements change over time. Towns and cities are not static. They may grow larger in response to urbanization or shrink due to lack of resources. As you study the history of a particular settlement, consider the factors that have caused the area to change.

Practice Test Items

27 As colonialism in West Africa ended, why did Benin become more urbanized than Sierra Leone?

   A Sierra Leone has a young population.

   B Sierra Leone is much smaller than Benin.

   C Sierra Leone does not have many natural resources.

   D <u>Sierra Leone has few highways and a poor transportation system.</u>

TEKS 6B

28 The city of Brasília was designed in 1957, and it has grown to 2.6 million people since then largely because it —

   A has a mild climate

   B <u>is the capital of Brazil</u>

   C has rich mineral deposits

   D is located near ocean trade routes

TEKS 6B

16

TEKS Test Prep Support

TEKS 7A

Construct and analyze population pyramids and use other data, graphics, and maps to describe the population characteristics of different societies and to predict future population trends.

What does it mean?

This supporting standard focuses on using population pyramids and other data to recognize and interpret patterns in population growth. These patterns, in turn, can provide information about the characteristics of the populations of nations at different levels of development. You can use this information to predict how populations will change in the future.

Practice Test Items

29

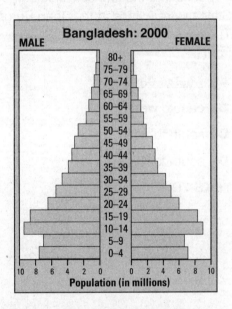

Based on the population pyramid, which statement was most likely true of Bangladesh in 2000?

A Demand for daycare centers increased drastically.

B The country had record numbers of retired citizens.

C High schools dealt with issues related to overcrowding.

D The country experienced a baby boom in the early 1950s.

TEKS 7A, TEKS 21A

30 Based on the population pyramid, what can you predict about Bangladesh in 2040?

A The country will need more colleges.

B The population of middle-aged people will expand.

C Most of the population will be under 10 years of age.

D The life expectancy of both males and females will decrease.

TEKS 7A, TEKS 21A

TEKS Test Prep Support

TEKS 7B

Explain how political, economic, social, and environmental push and pull factors and physical geography affect the routes and flows of human migration.

What does it mean?

This readiness standard analyzes why people move from one place to another. It also considers the physical factors that affect migration, such as mountains or rivers. To master this standard, you must be able to distinguish between push factors that cause people to move and pull factors that attract people to new places.

Practice Test Items

31 A family moves from a rural village to a nearby city in search of a better life and well-paying jobs. How would you classify their reason for moving?

   A a push factor motivated by politics

   B <u>a pull factor motivated by economics</u>

   C a push factor motivated by social concerns

   D a pull factor motivated by environmental issues

   TEKS 7B, TEKS 22C

32 Suppose that the first colonists in the United States were Asians, rather than Europeans. The flow of migration would likely have been from —

   A <u>west to east</u>

   B east to west

   C south to east

   D south to north

   TEKS 7B

TEKS Test Prep Support

TEKS 7C

Describe trends in world population growth and distribution.

What does it mean?
This readiness standard focuses on changes in human population. How many people inhabited the Earth in the past? How do these numbers compare to the current human population? Where do most people live and how will this change over time?

Practice Test Items

33

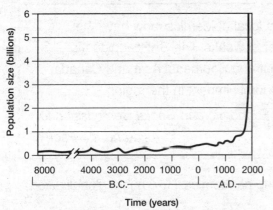

Which statement best describes the data in the graph?

A Human population fell dramatically following the last ice age.

B <u>Human population was relatively small until the Industrial Revolution.</u>

C Human population has leveled off since the beginning of the 21st century.

D Human population peaked early, then decreased as people formed permanent settlements.

TEKS 7C, TEKS 21A

34 Which statement about human population trends is true?

A Africa currently has the highest growth rate, but it will soon be surpassed by Oceania.

B Latin America is the most populous region, but its growth will slow in the near future.

C North America has the world's lowest growth rate, and its population is projected to steadily decline.

D <u>Asia has the largest population, and it is projected to remain most populous over the next few decades.</u>

TEKS 7C

TEKS Test Prep Support

TEKS 7D

Examine benefits and challenges of globalization, including connectivity, standard of living, pandemics, and loss of local culture.

What does it mean?
Globalization describes the global spread of ideas, culture, communications, and technology. This supporting standard analyzes the effects of globalization on different cultures. To master this standard, you must consider both the advantages and disadvantages of globalization.

Practice Test Items

35

> Infectious diseases, which could be contained as local epidemics, now have the potential to turn into global pandemics in a matter of weeks. The SARS epidemic spread across a large number of countries in East and Southeast Asia and Canada, resulting in loss of lives, and unprecedented economic impact in the region.
>
> —*Globalization and Health, United Nations Economic and Social Commission for Asia and the Pacific*

Globalization can worsen health issues by increasing pandemics. How might globalization benefit health issues?

A Access to the Internet allows for the sale of unregulated medicines.

B <u>Access to email increases communications between health professionals.</u>

C Multinational corporations give health benefits to all employees when they relocate to developing nations.

D Travel between countries can be easily controlled by using computers to track the movement of people.

TEKS 7D, TEKS 23B

---

36 A young woman of Canada's First Nations wants to maintain her cultural identity. The best measure she could take would be to —

A speak English at home

C pursue a degree in higher education

B move to a more populated province

D <u>interview an elder about family traditions</u>

TEKS 7D

TEKS Test Prep Support

TEKS 8A

Compare ways that humans depend on, adapt to, and modify the physical environment, including the influences of culture and technology.

What does it mean?
This readiness standard considers how people respond to their physical surroundings. People get important resources from the environment. They wear clothes and live in houses suited to different environmental conditions. In addition, people change the environment when they develop land for cities, farms, highways, and other uses.

Practice Test Items

37 How People Modify the Environment

Positive	Negative
Planting trees	_?_

Which human activity should be placed in the column about how people modify the environment in negative ways?

A Composting

B Littering

C Reclamation

D Recycling

TEKS 8A

38 An igloo is an adaptation to —

A pollution

B cold climates

C lack of resources

D crowded conditions

TEKS 8A

 GO ON

TEKS Test Prep Support

TEKS 8B

Describe the interaction between humans and the physical environment, and analyze the consequences of extreme weather and other natural disasters such as El Niño, floods, tsunamis, and volcanoes.

What does it mean?

This readiness standard focuses on how people interact with the environment. It also considers how the physical environment interacts with people. To master this standard, you must be familiar with the effects of a wide range of natural disasters.

Practice Test Items

39 Somalia experienced a severe famine in the early 1990s, resulting in the deaths of more than 300,000 people. The famine was caused by drought, but worsened by —

A <u>civil war</u>

B severe storms

C lack of international aid

D cultural resistance to accepting aid

TEKS 8B

40 What can you infer about an area that experiences seasonal monsoons and therefore has crippling floods?

A The area is situated far inland.

B The area is located at high latitudes.

C <u>The area also experiences crippling droughts.</u>

D Flooding generally occurs during the winter.

TEKS 8B

TEKS Test Prep Support

TEKS 8C

Evaluate the economic and political relationships between settlements and the environment, including sustainable development and renewable/non-renewable resources.

What does it mean?

This supporting standard asks you to evaluate how people make decisions about resource use. To master this standard, you must understand terms such as *sustainable development, renewable resource,* and *non-renewable resource.* Then, you can better analyze the economic and political reasons that guide resource use.

Practice Test Items

41 For the United States, one benefit of encouraging the development of renewable sources of energy is —

   A a reduction in the cost of energy

   B <u>less reliance on foreign sources of oil</u>

   C increased mining of domestic stores of fossil fuels

   D heavy reliance on resources that are replaced by artificial processes

TEKS 8C, TEKS 22C

42

> The city of Vancouver, British Columbia, has grown quickly in the past few decades. The growth of outlying suburbs often took place at the expense of forests, farms, and flood plains. In 1995, the Greater Vancouver Regional Board adopted a plan to manage growth. It involved turning suburbs into sustainable communities.

What is true of these sustainable communities?

   A Residents commute long distances.

   B <u>Residents live and work in the same community.</u>

   C Residents build their homes entirely of renewable resources.

   D All residents share ownership of the land on which the community is built.

TEKS 8C, TEKS 23B

TEKS Test Prep Support

TEKS 9A

Identify physical and/or human factors such as climate, vegetation, language, trade networks, political units, river systems, and religion that constitute a region.

What does it mean?

This readiness standard examines the factors used to determine regions, such as language, climate, and religion. Some of these factors may be shared by more than one region. But, in general, a region has a unique combination of characteristics that sets it apart from surrounding regions.

Practice Test Items

43

Languages of South America

Which region on the map has the least European influence?

A <u>central</u>   **C** southern

B eastern   **D** western

TEKS 9A, TEKS 21B

---

44 Note the regions on the map that speak European languages. Based on what you know about the countries from which these languages originated, you can infer that the regions with European languages likely share the same —

A climate   **C** trade networks

B <u>religion</u>   **D** vegetation

TEKS 9A, TEKS 21C

GO ON

TEKS Test Prep Support

TEKS 9B

Describe different types of regions, including formal, functional, and perceptual regions.

What does it mean?
This supporting standard focuses on how regions are categorized. For example, some regions are classified by their interconnectedness, while others are classified by cultural similarities. To master this standard, you must be able to distinguish between formal, functional, and perceptual regions.

Practice Test Items

45 A geographer places the United States in a formal region based on continental area and cultural styles. This formal region would also include —

   A Canada

   B Europe

   C Latin America

   D Southwest Asia

TEKS 9B, TEKS 22C

46 Which of the following is an example of a functional region?

   A a desert with a hot climate

   B a city and its interconnected suburbs

   C a part of the country characterized by tall grasses

   D an area with characteristics that are perceived by people in the same way

TEKS 9B, TEKS 22C

25

TEKS Test Prep Support

TEKS 10A

Describe the forces that determine the distribution of goods and services in free enterprise, socialist, and communist economic systems.

What does it mean?
This supporting standard focuses on how products and services are distributed in different types of economic systems. To master this standard, you must compare and contrast the characteristics of free enterprise, socialist, and communist economic systems.

Practice Test Items

47

> After the Soviet collapse in 1991, Russia took steps to change its economic system. In January 1992, it removed the price controls that had been set by the Soviet government on goods sold within the country. That same year, Russia began to sell government-owned businesses to individuals and private companies.

In the early 1990s, Russia moved from a —

A socialist system to a communist system

B free enterprise system to a socialist system

C socialist system to a free enterprise system

D communist system to a free enterprise system

TEKS 10A, TEKS 23B

48 Who owns most of the resources, technology, and businesses in a free enterprise system?

A local government

B federal government

C private individuals

D nonprofit organizations

TEKS 10A, TEKS 22C

26

© Houghton Mifflin Harcourt Publishing Company

GO ON

TEKS Test Prep Support

TEKS 10B

Classify where specific countries fall along the economic spectrum between free enterprise and communism.

What does it mean?

Economic systems fall along the range of loosely regulated to tightly controlled. This supporting standard asks you to rank countries according to where they would fall on a scale between free enterprise and communism. As you study different countries, take notes about their economic systems to help you better classify them.

Practice Test Items

49 On a scale of 1 to 10, with 1 being free enterprise and 10 being communism, the former Soviet Union would be classified as —

A 1

B 3

C 5

D <u>10</u>

TEKS 10B

50

1	
2	
3	
4	
5	

On this scale, 1 represents free enterprise and 5 represents communism. In which box would you place the United States?

A <u>Box 1</u>

B Box 3

C Box 4

D Box 5

TEKS 10B

GO ON

27

TEKS Test Prep Support

TEKS 10C

Compare the ways people satisfy their basic needs through the production of goods and services such as subsistence agriculture versus commercial agriculture or cottage industries versus commercial industries.

What does it mean?

This readiness standard analyzes how people make a living. Countries have different levels of economic development, and these different levels are reflected in how people work. For example, people in developing nations are more likely to practice subsistence agriculture than are people in more developed nations.

Practice Test Items

51 How does subsistence agriculture compare to commercial agriculture?

   A Technology plays a larger role in subsistence agriculture than in commercial agriculture.

   B Subsistence agriculture generally affects a very large area, whereas commercial agriculture affects a local area.

   C Subsistence agriculture is usually associated with capitalist systems, and commercial agriculture is usually associated with communist systems.

   D <u>In subsistence agriculture, little food is left over to sell to others. In commercial agriculture, crops are grown to be sold to others.</u>

   TEKS 10C

52 Which is an example of a cottage industry?

   A A factory builds and distributes car parts globally.

   B A woman teaches high school students at the local school.

   C <u>A family sets up a woodshop in their garage to make and sell furniture.</u>

   D A rancher buys 2 million hectares of land for grazing cattle, which are then sold at a market in a large city.

   TEKS 10C

TEKS Test Prep Support

TEKS 10D

Compare global trade patterns over time and examine the implications of globalization, including outsourcing and free trade zones.

What does it mean?

This supporting standard focuses on changes in trade patterns over time. For example, trade patterns were once largely determined by geography. Advances in technology made it possible to expand trade routes. The standard also considers the effects of globalization on trading partners.

Practice Test Items

53

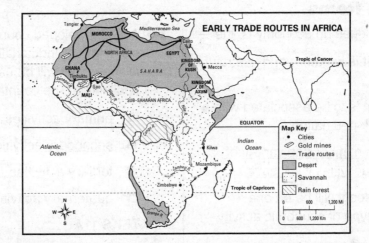

What can you conclude from this map?

A West Africa was a major exporter of gold.

B Traders were reluctant to cross the Sahara desert.

C Most early African trade routes flowed from south to north.

D Africa did not have thriving trade routes until relatively recently.

TEKS 10D, TEKS 21C

---

54 Outsourcing occurs when a company hires an outside business to provide a service to its customers or to do specialized work. The company can save time and money by outsourcing. However, one disadvantage of outsourcing is —

A hidden costs related to paid benefits

B less direct oversight on a product or service

C lack of technology to facilitate communications

D less capital available to use for other purposes

TEKS 10D

TEKS Test Prep Support

TEKS 11A

Understand the connections between levels of development and economic activities (primary, secondary, tertiary, and quaternary).

What does it mean?

This supporting standard relates the level of development of a country to one of four economic activities. The four economic activities (primary, secondary, tertiary, and quaternary) describe how materials are gathered and processed into goods or how services are delivered to consumers. To master this standard, you must have a thorough knowledge of levels of development and the four economic activities.

Practice Test Items

55 The more developed an economy is, the —

   A less likely it is to gather and use raw materials

   B less likely it is to be associated with a more developed nation

   C <u>greater the number and variety of economic activities it will have</u>

   D more focused it will be on one particular type of economic activity

   TEKS 11A

56 A less developed country is taking the first steps toward industrialization. It is building factories that will be used to manufacture appliances. The country is moving into —

   A primary activities

   B <u>secondary activities</u>

   C tertiary activities

   D quaternary activities

   TEKS 11A

GO ON

TEKS Test Prep Support

TEKS 11B

Identify the factors affecting the location of different types of economic activities, including subsistence and commercial agriculture, manufacturing, and service industries.

What does it mean?

This supporting standard considers where economic activities are located and why the activities are found in particular places. Certain manufacturing industries, for example, are located along rivers or lakes because they need ready access to water supplies. To master this standard, think about the resources needed by different economic activities. How might these needs affect decisions concerning where to locate a farm or factory?

Practice Test Items

57 A woman plans to start a computer-repair business. She wants to work mainly with large companies that use hundreds of computers on a daily basis. Which location would guarantee the greatest success for her business?

  A a rural village

  B <u>an urban district</u>

  C an undeveloped forest

  D a suburban neighborhood

TEKS 11B

58 A subsistence farmer in the Amazon River basin in Brazil practices slash-and-burn farming. Where is he most likely to locate his crops?

  A near a road for easy access to markets

  B near a city for easy access to equipment

  C near his home for easy access to his fields

  D <u>near the forest for easy access to newly cleared land</u>

TEKS 11B

TEKS Test Prep Support

TEKS 11C

Assess how changes in climate, resources, and infrastructure (technology, transportation, and communication) affect the location and patterns of economic activities.

What does it mean?

This readiness standard considers how changes in certain factors might in turn cause changes in economic activities. For example, a new highway might connect a once-isolated area to a large city, allowing the area to more easily transport goods to the city. In this case, a change in infrastructure causes a change in a pattern of economic activity.

Practice Test Items

59

> The economy of the Maldives has changed over the years. Fishing for species such as tuna, marlin, and sharks was once the main economic activity. The fishing industry is still a large part of the economy—it provides one fourth of the jobs—but it has been replaced in importance by tourism.

What can you infer about tourism in the Maldives?

A It is less lucrative than fishing.

B <u>It brings in more money annually than fishing.</u>

C Unlike fishing, it is a seasonal economic activity.

D Unlike fishing, it is based on renewable resources.

TEKS 11C, TEKS 23B

60

> Jamaica was originally a plantation economy that depended on the sale of bananas and sugar for its livelihood. Then it turned to the mining and processing of bauxite (aluminum ore) to make the country less dependent on agriculture. Today, this resource is mainly an export that is shipped elsewhere for industrial use.

Why might Jamaica want to be less dependent on agriculture?

A The demand for food has decreased in recent years.

B Agriculture causes more pollution than does mining.

C The climate in Jamaica has gotten much colder in recent decades.

D <u>Income from agriculture can vary greatly depending on the weather.</u>

TEKS 11C, TEKS 23B

Name _____ Date _____

TEKS Test Prep Support

TEKS 12A

Analyze how the creation, distribution, and management of key natural resources affect the location and patterns of movement of products, money, and people.

What does it mean?
This readiness standard analyzes how the presence of important natural resources influences the movement of products, people, and money. As you study different regions, note their most important resources and consider how these resources affect both people and economic activities.

Practice Test Items

61

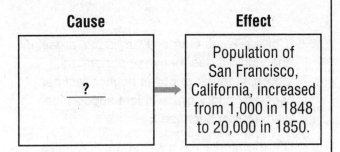

Cause	Effect
?	Population of San Francisco, California, increased from 1,000 in 1848 to 20,000 in 1850.

What cause should be placed in the graphic organizer to explain why the population of San Francisco increased so sharply?

A End of Civil War

B Discovery of gold

C Immigration of Native Americans

D Discovery of pass across Appalachian Mountains

TEKS 12A

62 Africa's great mineral wealth has not translated into prosperity for most of its population partly because the resources were —

A hard to access

B nonrenewable and soon depleted

C not in high demand because they were priced too high

D exported elsewhere throughout the 19th and 20 centuries

TEKS 12A

TEKS Test Prep Support

TEKS 12B

Evaluate the geographic and economic impact of policies related to the development, use, and scarcity of natural resources such as regulations of water.

What does it mean?

This supporting standard focuses on government policies that manage the use of natural resources, such as water, air, and land. Some of these policies protect the quality of the resource, such as laws that monitor the amount of pollution that can be released into the environment. Other laws oversee how a resource can be used—some land, for example, is set aside for preservation—or how much of a resource can be used by any one party. The latter is particularly true of water rights in arid or semi-arid areas.

Practice Test Items

63

> Nine states in the western United States are governed by a doctrine called "prior appropriation," which basically means "first come, first served." For example, a rancher who has had water rights since 1893 will get his or her share of water before a rancher who has had water rights since 1894.

What is one disadvantage of the doctrine of prior appropriation?

A It is not widely used in the West.

B It has not been thoroughly tested over time.

C It does not consider whether one water use is more beneficial than another.

D It is no longer relevant in the West because the area has plentiful water and is no longer prone to droughts.

TEKS 12B, TEKS 23B

64 China's Three Gorges Dam is the largest in the world. It has many supporters and critics. In terms of how it might affect her work, a factory owner might support the dam mainly because it —

A created a reservoir some 400 miles long

B improved irrigation to agricultural areas

C forced millions of people to relocate to new areas

D improved the reliability of electricity throughout China

TEKS 12B

GO ON

TEKS Test Prep Support

TEKS 13B

Compare maps of voting patterns or political boundaries to make inferences about the distribution of political power.

What does it mean?

This supporting standard asks you to make inferences about political power by comparing patterns you see in maps. These patterns can help you to better understand changes in political power over time. To master this standard, analyze changes in voting patterns or political boundaries as you study maps.

Practice Test Items

65

Maps of Changing Borders of Poland, 1763 through 1919

How would you describe Poland's political power during the time period shown on the maps?

A steady

B varying

C declining

D increasing

TEKS 13B, TEKS 13A

---

66 Which statement best describes the maps?

A Poland and Prussia were close allies.

B Poland lost power as Russia gained power.

C Austria was not a political player during that period.

D The two biggest powers in that period were Poland and the Ottoman Empire.

TEKS 13B, TEKS 13A

TEKS Test Prep Support

TEKS 14B

Compare how democracy, dictatorship, monarchy, republic, theocracy, and totalitarian systems operate in specific countries.

What does it mean?

This supporting standard focuses on different types of political systems. To master this standard, you must know the characteristics of political systems ranging from democracies to totalitarian systems. As you study different countries, compare the extent to which their governments share power with their citizens.

Practice Test Items

67

Characteristics of Political System

North Korea	Saudi Arabia
• Individual or group holds complete political power • No free elections	• Ruling family headed by king or queen • King or queen holds political power • Political power may or may not be shared with citizens

How do the political systems of North Korea and Saudi Arabia compare?

A North Korea is a monarchy. Saudi Arabia is a republic.

B North Korea is a democracy. Saudi Arabia is a theocracy.

C North Korea is a dictatorship. Saudi Arabia is a monarchy.

D North Korea is a republic. Saudi Arabia is a totalitarian system.

TEKS 14B, TEKS 21A

---

68 In Western Europe, citizens hold political power either directly or through elected representatives. The countries of Western Europe are —

A democracies

C monarchies

B dictatorships

D theocracies

TEKS 14B

GO ON

TEKS Test Prep Support

TEKS 14C

Analyze the human and physical factors that influence the power to control territory and resources, create conflict/war, and impact international political relations of sovereign nations such as China, the United States, Japan, and Russia and organized nation groups such as the United Nations (UN) and the European Union (EU).

What does it mean?

This readiness standard asks you to analyze the factors that affect relationships between powerful nations and nation groups. Why do some countries go to war while others form long-term alliances? As you study the countries and groups mentioned in the standard, it's helpful to consider how the history of a country might have an impact on its interactions with other countries.

Practice Test Items

69 The European Union (EU) was created mainly to —

A build a strong military

B <u>promote economic growth</u>

C prevent religious persecution

D protect environmental interests

TEKS 14C

70 Between 2004 and 2007, many Eastern European countries joined the EU. This created some friction because these countries were —

A <u>former communist regimes with little democratic experience</u>

B far more liberal and open to change than existing EU members

C mainly Muslim nations with different outlooks on human rights

D far more prosperous than their Western European counterparts

TEKS 14C

GO ON

TEKS Test Prep Support

TEKS 15A

Identify and give examples of different points of view that influence the development of public policies and decision-making processes on local, state, national, and international levels.

What does it mean?

This supporting standard examines how public policies come about. As you read about public policies and decision-making processes, ask questions such as, "What is the purpose of this policy? Who supports it and why? Who is against it and why? What process did lawmakers use to make a decision about the policy?"

Practice Test Items

71

> In 1997, the UN held a convention in Kyoto, Japan, to discuss climate change. The conference wrote the Kyoto Protocol, guidelines for developed countries to reduce greenhouse gas emissions. In time, 165 nations signed the treaty. The United States signed the treaty, but the Senate did not ratify it.

The U.S. Senate refused to ratify the Kyoto Protocol because opponents of the protocol believed that it would —

A <u>harm American businesses</u>

B contribute to global warming

C lead to increased reliance on fossil fuels

D discourage scientific research on the issue

TEKS 15A, TEKS 23B

72 A group of city residents is against a proposal to build a large apartment complex for university students in a residential neighborhood made up mainly of families. To express their views, they are most likely to attend a —

A <u>city council meeting</u>

B committee meeting of state representatives

C session of U.S. Congress

D gathering of delegates from the United Nations

TEKS 15A

GO ON

TEKS Test Prep Support

TEKS 15B

Explain how citizenship practices, public policies, and decision making may be influenced by cultural beliefs, including nationalism and patriotism.

What does it mean?
This supporting standard focuses on how cultural beliefs, such as nationalism and patriotism, affect both governments and their citizens. To master this standard, you must understand the meanings of terms such as *nationalism* and *patriotism* and relate these meanings to citizenship practices, public policies, and decision-making processes.

Practice Test Items

73 Which of the following is an example of a U.S. citizen engaged in a patriotic act?

A A woman volunteers to help orphans in Peru.

B A girl pursues her dream of becoming a veterinarian.

C A man stands during the playing of the national anthem.

D A boy designs a paper airplane that can fly long distances.

TEKS 15B, TEKS 22C

74 World War II was caused in part by strong nationalistic feelings and bitter resentment on the part of —

A England

B Germany

C Israel

D Mexico

TEKS 15B, TEKS 22C

GO ON

39

TEKS Test Prep Support

TEKS 16A

Describe distinctive cultural patterns and landscapes associated with different places in Texas, the United States, and other regions of the world and how these patterns influenced the processes of innovation and diffusion.

What does it mean?

Innovation involves taking existing technology and resources and creating something new. Diffusion involves the spread of ideas or behaviors from one culture to another. This supporting standard asks you to describe how cultural elements contribute to the processes of innovation and diffusion.

Practice Test Items

75 Texas has a large population of Spanish-speaking residents because it —

  A <u>borders Mexico</u>

  B was once claimed by France

  C was settled by Native Americans

  D has a strong trading relationship with Cuba

TEKS 16A

76 The Hittites were an ancient people who established an empire in the Fertile Crescent. What innovation is associated with the Hittites?

  A They were brave hunters who invented fire.

  B They were great scholars who invented writing.

  C <u>They were a warlike culture that developed iron weapons.</u>

  D They were an organized society that developed structured government.

TEKS 16A, TEKS 22C

 GO ON

TEKS Test Prep Support

TEKS 16B

Describe elements of culture, including language, religion, beliefs and customs, institutions, and technologies.

What does it mean?

Culture is the total knowledge, attitudes, and behaviors shared by and passed on by the members of a specific group. This readiness standard asks you to consider the elements that make up culture. As you read about different cultures, note the characteristics that make each culture unique.

Practice Test Items

77 A Southern drawl is an example of —

A <u>a dialect found in a certain region</u>

B a new language related to migration

C an evolved language with strong Sanskrit roots

D a blended language associated with trade routes

TEKS 16B

78

Types of Religions			
Animistic	**Monotheistic**	**Polytheistic**	**Traditional**

In which category would you classify Islam?

A animistic

B <u>monotheistic</u>

C polytheistic

D traditional

TEKS 16B

TEKS Test Prep Support

TEKS 16C

Explain ways various groups of people perceive the characteristics of their own and other cultures, places, and regions differently.

What does it mean?

This supporting standard analyzes how different cultures and places view one another. Recall that culture ties people to one group and separates them from other groups. Although there is much interaction and respect across cultures, there is also a tendency to view one's own culture as preferable to others.

Practice Test Items

79 How is a citizen of Quebec most likely to perceive himself?

A as an immigrant

B <u>as a French Canadian</u>

C as a resident of the Atlantic Provinces

D as a member of the Dominion of Canada

TEKS 16C

80 The Palestine Liberation Organization was formed in 1964 to regain the land of Palestinian Arabs. A citizen of Israel is likely to view this organization as —

A an ally

B a humanitarian group

C a peace-keeping force

D <u>a terrorist group</u>

TEKS 16C

42

TEKS Test Prep Support

TEKS 16D

Compare life in a variety of urban and rural areas in the world to evaluate political, economic, social, and environmental changes.

What does it mean?

This supporting standard asks you to evaluate how change has an impact to life in different rural and urban areas around the world. This change can be political, economic, social, or environmental. To master this standard, try to put yourself in the place of an urban or rural person in the region you are studying.

Practice Test Items

81 Djibouti, located on the Gulf of Aden in East Africa, is working to establish itself as a major international shipping center. How will this change impact the city and set it apart from many other areas in Africa?

   A It will encourage more educated citizens to leave the city.

   B It will make the economy more unstable and place jobs at risk.

   C <u>It will diversify the economy and give people more opportunities.</u>

   D It will improve political stability by providing more money to the ruling party.

TEKS 16D

82

> Because of its rapidly growing population, China adopted a policy of one child per family in 1979. The country also outlawed early marriage. A man must be 22 and a woman must be 20 before they can marry. Those policies have reduced China's birthrate dramatically.

What is the main reason this policy has run into opposition?

   A Rural areas are underpopulated compared to urban areas.

   B Large families are viewed as status symbols in urban areas.

   C <u>Rural families feel that they need more than one child to help work their farms.</u>

   D Urban families feel that China has enough resources to support unlimited growth.

TEKS 16D, TEKS 23B

GO ON

TEKS Test Prep Support

TEKS 17A

Describe and compare patterns of culture such as language, religion, land use, education, and customs that make specific regions of the world distinctive.

What does it mean?

This readiness standard focuses on the cultural elements that distinguish one region from another. It asks you to look for patterns in these elements. As you read about different regions, carefully study maps, diagrams, charts, and other types of graphics; they can often help you recognize cultural patterns.

Practice Test Items

83

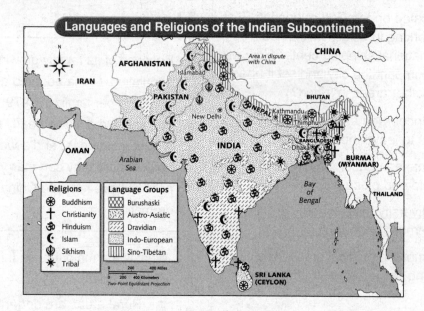

Languages and Religions of the Indian Subcontinent

According to this map, in central India, you would most likely encounter a person who is —

A a Hindu

B a Muslim

C speaking Burushaski

D speaking a Sino-Tibetan language

TEKS 17A, TEKS 21C

---

84 Based on the map, you can infer that Europe had a strong influence on India because —

A Christianity is the main religion of India

B most Indians speak the Sino-Tibetan language

C the Indo-European language is very widespread

D most Indians practice Buddhism, which originated in Europe

TEKS 17A, TEKS 21C

Name _____ Date _____

TEKS Test Prep Support

TEKS 17B

Describe major world religions, including animism, Buddhism, Christianity, Hinduism, Islam, Judaism, and Sikhism, and their spatial distribution.

What does it mean?

This supporting standard asks you to describe the world's main religions. What are their characteristics? Where are they found? To master this standard, it's helpful to visualize where a particular religion originated and its pattern of diffusion from its place of origin.

Practice Test Items

85

Major Characteristics of ___?___
• Roots go back about 4,000 years
• Considered oldest monotheistic religion
• Most sacred text is the Torah

Which religion is described in the chart?

A Christianity

B Buddhism

C <u>Judaism</u>

D Sikhism

TEKS 17B, TEKS 21A

86 Islam originated in Arabia and spread mainly throughout —

A Australia

B <u>the Middle East</u>

C North America

D South America

TEKS 17B

GO ON

TEKS Test Prep Support

TEKS 17C

Compare economic, political, or social opportunities in different cultures for women, ethnic and religious minorities, and other underrepresented populations.

What does it mean?

This supporting standard focuses on how minorities and other underrepresented populations fare in different cultures. It analyzes quality of life issues in terms of economic, political, and social opportunities. As you study different regions, take note of the opportunities that exist for underrepresented populations. Be aware that some cultures are characterized by lack of opportunities for women, minorities, and other groups.

Practice Test Items

87

> Eating in restaurants in Eastern Mediterranean countries is not as common as in the United States. Some Arab restaurants have separate sections for men and women. Arab cafes serving coffee and tea are generally for men only.

A woman in the United States would have —

A less social, political, and economic opportunities than a woman in an Eastern Mediterranean country

B more social, political, and economic opportunities than a woman in an Eastern Mediterranean country

C exactly the same amount of social, political, and economic opportunities as a woman in an Eastern Mediterranean country

D nearly the same amount of social, political, and economic opportunities as a woman in an Eastern Mediterranean country

TEKS 17C, TEKS 21A

88 During the 2000 Olympics in Sydney, Australia, Aboriginal protestors set up a tent embassy to inform the world of their struggle to —

A win the right to vote

B get religious freedom

C regain ancestral lands taken by white settlers

D arrange the return of mixed-race children who were given up for adoption against their will

TEKS 17C

GO ON

TEKS Test Prep Support

TEKS 17D

Evaluate the experiences and contributions of diverse groups to multicultural societies.

What does it mean?
This supporting standard analyzes two things: what type of experience diverse groups have in multicultural societies and what contributions these groups make to their respective societies. Many countries, including the United States, are multicultural. When you study multicultural societies, note the experiences of new immigrants and how cultural elements spread from one group to another.

Practice Test Items

89

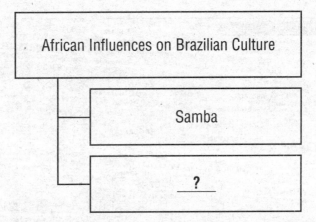

What African influence on Brazilian culture completes the diagram?

A *Banya*

B Capoeira

C Gaucho

D Sushi

TEKS 17D

---

90 Unlike those who had come earlier, immigrants who came to the United States in the late 20th century were —

A reluctant to give up their traditions and beliefs in order to assimilate

B eager to undergo "Americanization" and blend in with their new country

C mainly from southern and Eastern Europe, in search of economic opportunities

D hostile to 19th-century immigrants who retained strong ties to their cultural heritage

TEKS 17D

GO ON

TEKS Test Prep Support

TEKS 18A

Analyze cultural changes in specific regions caused by migration, war, trade, innovations, and diffusion.

What does it mean?

This readiness standard focuses on how important events and processes can cause cultures to change. For example, war can bring political, economic, religious, and social change to a country. As you read about migrations, wars, and other events, think about how they had an impact on different cultural elements in the region you are studying.

Practice Test Items

91

According to the map, what can you infer about how Europe looked before the Cold War ended?

A Most Northern European countries were communist regimes.

C <u>Most Eastern European countries were republics of the Soviet Union.</u>

B Most Western European countries were part of East Germany.

D Most Southern European countries were not considered part of Europe until after the 1980s.

TEKS 18A, TEKS 13A

---

92 Using the map, what is the best description for how Europe changed after the Cold War ended?

A Most Western European countries embraced communism.

C Most Central European countries became satellite states of Russia.

B <u>Most Eastern European countries became independent nations.</u>

D Most Northern European countries broke away from East Germany.

TEKS 18A, TEKS 21B

GO ON ▶

TEKS Test Prep Support

TEKS 18B

Assess causes, effects, and perceptions of conflicts between groups of people, including modern genocides and terrorism.

What does it mean?
Genocide is the deliberate destruction of an ethnic or cultural group. Terrorism is the unlawful use of or threatened use of violence for political or social ends. In this supporting standard, you must analyze modern examples of genocide and terrorism, and assess their causes and effects.

Practice Test Items

93 Airline security in the United States has become much tighter since 2001, as a direct result of terrorist attacks by —

    A <u>al-Qaeda</u>

    B Pakistani extremists

    C Chechen separatists

    D militant domestic groups

TEKS 18B

94 Serbia views Kosovo as a sacred part of its heritage. In the 1990s, it attempted to assert control over Kosovo by —

    A <u>wiping out Muslim Albanians and their culture</u>

    B backing Croats in the war against Bosnia's Muslims

    C joining with the United Nations to stop ethnic cleansing in Kosovo

    D forming the Kosovo Liberation Army to carry out attacks against Muslims

TEKS 18B

TEKS Test Prep Support

TEKS 18C

Identify examples of cultures that maintain traditional ways, including traditional economies.

What does it mean?

This supporting standard asks you to identify cultures that carry on traditional ways. To master this standard, you must recognize the characteristics of traditional cultures. You may find it helpful to focus on native cultures as you study different regions.

Practice Test Items

95 Which is an example of a person engaged in a traditional economy?

A An African opens an insurance office in a busy city.

B A Peruvian barters a woven mat for freshly caught fish.

C An Indian designs parts for airplanes in a research facility.

D A Russian sells handmade pastries from a vendor cart on a sidewalk.

TEKS 18C

96

Characteristics of __?__
• Constitutional monarchy
• Main ethnic group is *Bhote*
• Official religion is Buddhism
• Artisans known for metal bells and intricate wooden sculptures
• Famous for archery competitions

Which traditional culture is described in the chart?

A Bhutan

B Kurds

C Maori

D Masai

TEKS 18C

© Houghton Mifflin Harcourt Publishing Company

TEKS Test Prep Support

TEKS 18D

Evaluate the spread of cultural traits to find examples of cultural convergence and divergence such as the spread of democratic ideas, U.S.-based fast-food franchises, the English language, technology, or global sports.

What does it mean?

Cultural convergence describes how cultures become more alike over time. Cultural divergence describes how cultures become less alike over time. This supporting standard asks you to evaluate the spread of cultural traits to identify examples of cultural convergence and divergence.

Practice Test Items

97 Which of the following is likely to encourage cultural divergence?

   A <u>geographic isolation</u>

   B access to technology

   C improved transportation

   D improved communications

TEKS 18D, TEKS 22C

98 Which is most likely to increase the demand for U.S. fast-food franchises in a South American town?

   A civil wars

   B history textbooks

   C political speeches

   D <u>televisions</u>

TEKS 18D

GO ON

51

TEKS Test Prep Support

TEKS 19A

Evaluate the significance of major technological innovations in the areas of transportation and energy that have been used to modify the physical environment.

What does it mean?
This readiness standard asks you to evaluate the impact of advances in transportation and energy. What was their purpose? How did they change the physical environment? As you study different regions, pay close attention to information about railroads, canals, power plants, and other technological innovations that affect people and places.

Practice Test Items

99

North America's most important deepwater ship route—the St. Lawrence Seaway—was completed in the 1950s, as a joint project of the United States and Canada. The seaway connects the Great Lakes to the Atlantic Ocean by way of the St. Lawrence River. Ships are raised and lowered some 600 feet by a series of locks, sections of a waterway with closed gates where water levels are raised or lowered.

What was the purpose of the St. Lawrence Seaway?

A It opened up the Northwest to settlers.

B It defined the political border between the United States and Canada.

C It was the first navigable water link between the Atlantic and the Great Lakes.

D It allowed huge vessels to sail into the industrial and agriculture heartland of North America.

TEKS 19A, TEKS 21A

---

100 What was one impact of the explosion of the Chernobyl power plant in 1986?

A Costs related to the disaster reached $300 million.

B Some 100,000 square miles of land were contaminated.

C Approximately 250,000 people resettled in the area by 2000.

D The plant was shut down permanently and quit producing electricity.

TEKS 19A

52

TEKS Test Prep Support

TEKS 19B

Analyze ways technological innovations such as air conditioning and desalinization have allowed humans to adapt to places.

What does it mean?

This supporting standard focuses on how technology affects where people can live. For example, air conditioning and desalinization allow people to live in harsh climates that might otherwise be inhabitable. To master this standard, think about where and when people might use these innovations, and how these innovations affect or might affect your own life.

Practice Test Items

101 Which area is most likely to build a desalinization plant?

A a hot city near a river

B a wet city near a forest

C <u>a dry city near an ocean</u>

B a cold city near a mountain

TEKS 19B

102

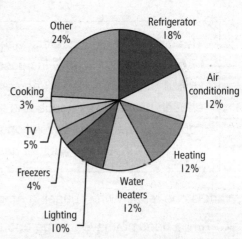

The graph shows typical energy consumption for a household in a moderate climate. A household in a hot climate would most likely see an increase in the percentage of energy used for —

A <u>air conditioning</u>

B heating

C lighting

D TV

TEKS 19B

GO ON

TEKS Test Prep Support

TEKS 19C

Examine the environmental, economic, and social impacts of advances in technology on agriculture and natural resources.

What does it mean?
This readiness standard assesses the impacts of technology used to produce food or obtain and use natural resources. It specifically examines the environmental, economic, and social impacts of these types of technology. As you read about this subject, keep in mind that there are both benefits and costs involved in using technology.

Practice Test Items

103

> The Green Revolution refers to the period beginning around 1950, wherein new technologies significantly increased crop yields. For example, before 1940, the United States imported 50 percent of its wheat. By 1960, it was producing enough wheat for its needs and still had wheat left over to export to other countries. The Green Revolution was hailed as a way to end global hunger— particularly in Africa—but that has not been the case, due to a variety of factors.

What is one reason why hunger in Africa did not end following the Green Revolution?

A Africa does not have a large enough population to grow its own food.

B The population of Africa had grown faster than the ability of farmers to produce food.

C <u>Political instability and lack of infrastructure have disrupted the distribution of food in Africa.</u>

D High crop yields reached during the peak of the Green Revolution declined due to climate change.

TEKS 19C, TEKS 21B

---

104 Fossil fuels are an important natural resource used by countries around the world, but using fossil fuels does have a downside. Burning fossil fuels to power vehicles causes —

A eutrophication

B forest fires

C ozone depletion

D <u>smog</u>

TEKS 19C

54

TEKS Test Prep Support

TEKS 20A

Describe the impact of new information technologies such as the Internet, Global Positioning System (GPS), or Geographic Information Systems (GIS).

What does it mean?

This supporting standard asks you to describe how cutting-edge technology has affected modern society. As you read about these technologies, think about their different applications. What are they used for? Who uses them? How have they affected everyday life?

Practice Test Items

105 A city wants to determine the best location for a landfill. It is creating a composite map based on a terrain map, a land-use map, a road map, and 3-D images of groundwater reservoirs. What technology is it relying on to create the composite map?

   A the Internet

   B Global Positioning System

   C <u>Geographic Information Systems</u>

   D Geostationary Operational Environmental Satellites

TEKS 20A

106 Which type of technology would most likely enable a geographer to find her way out of a wilderness area after tracking a grizzly bear?

   A the Internet

   B <u>Global Positioning System</u>

   C Geographic Information Systems

   D Geostationary Operational Environmental Satellites

TEKS 20A

TEKS Test Prep Support

TEKS 20B

Examine the economic, environmental, and social effects of technology such as medical advancements or changing trade patterns on societies at different levels of development.

What does it mean?
This supporting standard analyzes how advances in medicine affect developing and developed nations. It also examines the effects of changes in trade patterns on these nations. In both cases, you are asked to focus specifically on economic, environmental, and social effects.

Practice Test Items

107 A developing country is plagued by malaria. A vaccine for malaria is distributed throughout the country. What will most likely happen next?

   A The country's birthrate will decrease.

   B The country's mortality rate will increase.

   C <u>The country's infant mortality rate will decrease.</u>

   D The country's rate of natural increase will remain the same.

TEKS 20B, TEKS 22C

108 A developed nation has a relatively high mortality rate. What can you infer about the nation?

   A Because of lack of medical technology, many people are dying.

   B Because it is a developed nation, it has a young population subject to disease.

   C Because it is a developed nation, it has a high birthrate and therefore a high infant mortality rate.

   D <u>Because of advancements in medical technology, it has many elderly people who are pushing up the mortality rate.</u>

TEKS 20B

56

Grade 9 World Geography
Practice Tests 1 and 2

Practice Test 1

1 Which two languages are spoken most frequently in United States?

A Spanish and English

B French and Spanish

C German and English

D Chinese and Spanish

2

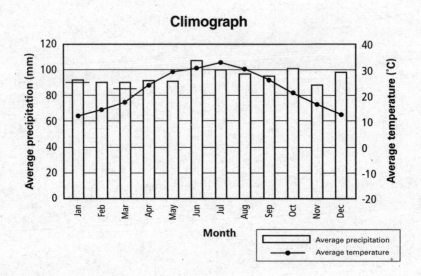

Climograph

Which of the following biomes does the climograph represent?

A savanna

B temperate forest

C tropical rain forest

D desert and dry shrub

GO ON

58

3 Which of the following shows the correct sequence in the formation of a hurricane?

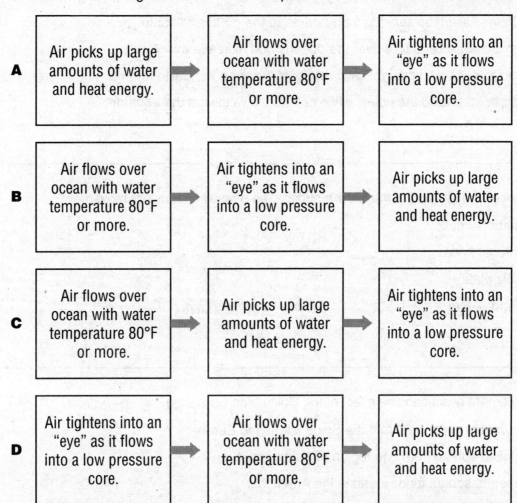

A   Air picks up large amounts of water and heat energy. → Air flows over ocean with water temperature 80°F or more. → Air tightens into an "eye" as it flows into a low pressure core.

B   Air flows over ocean with water temperature 80°F or more. → Air tightens into an "eye" as it flows into a low pressure core. → Air picks up large amounts of water and heat energy.

C   Air flows over ocean with water temperature 80°F or more. → Air picks up large amounts of water and heat energy. → Air tightens into an "eye" as it flows into a low pressure core.

D   Air tightens into an "eye" as it flows into a low pressure core. → Air flows over ocean with water temperature 80°F or more. → Air picks up large amounts of water and heat energy.

GO ON

4 What happens as wind currents move across regions?

A The Polar Easterlies serve to warm areas to the north and south.

B Air temperatures equalize over the oceans and increase over land.

C Air currents move in straight lines along latitudes as the Earth rotates.

D Hot air flows toward the poles, while cold air flows toward the equator.

5 Which causes the shaping of the Earth's surface, as a result of constant movement?

A gravitational pulls

B centrifugal force

C tectonic plates

D the Ring of Fire

6 Which statement describes one effect of the Columbian Exchange?

A Trade routes expanded from the Spice Islands to Europe.

B Buddhism spread from one region of Asia to another.

C Europeans sought foods found in the Americas.

D Silk became China's most valuable export.

GO ON

7

Major Sectors of the U.S. Economy

	Agriculture	Manufacturing	Services
1900	38%	36%	27%
1950	12%	41%	47%
2000	2%	35%	73%

Source: Historical Statistics of the United States: U.S. Bureau of Labor Statistics

Based on the information presented in the table, which statement best explains the change in economic indicators for the United States?

A The Unites States became less developed as the agriculture sector declined.

B Newly industrialized areas grew while agriculture declined in rural areas.

C Social and economic indicators recognized the importance of manufacturing.

D The service and manufacturing sectors outpaced agriculture as the country grew.

---

8 What is one way society benefits from the advanced technology that reduces carbon dioxide emissions?

A a potential increase in greenhouse gases

B a reduction in the effects of global warming

C an increase in industrial use of fossil fuels

D an acceleration of the global greenhouse effect

9

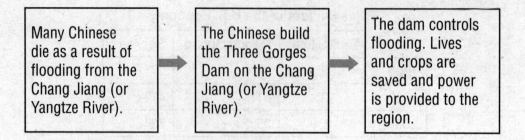

| Many Chinese die as a result of flooding from the Chang Jiang (or Yangtze River). | → | The Chinese build the Three Gorges Dam on the Chang Jiang (or Yangtze River). | → | The dam controls flooding. Lives and crops are saved and power is provided to the region. |

Building the Three Gorges Dam is an example of —

A people shaping their environment

B nature directing political decisions

C society limiting use of physical features

D natural resources becoming exhausted

10

> Under the rule of the Soviet government, the economy was controlled by the communist government. Since the fall of the Soviet Union, Russia and the other republics that once made up the Soviet Union have tried to stabilize their economies. Russia, for example, has slowly moved toward a market economy.

In allowing for a market economy, Russia is moving from what once was a communist economic system to one that allows the privatization of businesses known as —

A free enterprise

B a service industry

C dominant sectors

D supply and demand

GO ON

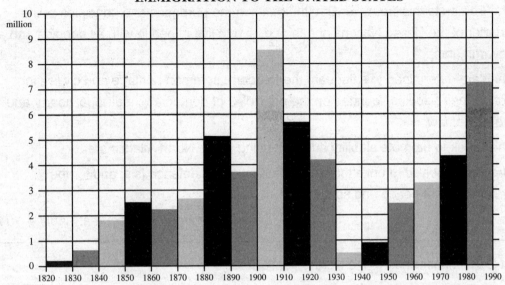

IMMIGRATION TO THE UNITED STATES

Consider the information presented in the graph. Which statement would be an accurate description of urban immigrant life in the United States in 1910?

A Though immigrants flocked to the cities, they needed to move to rural areas in the Midwest in order to practice their traditions.

B Between 1860 and 1900, some 14 million immigrants brought their native languages and traditions to the United States.

C Many immigrants believed the streets of the United States were paved with gold, so they were willing to give up their native culture.

D Native traditions once found in cities disappeared around the end of World War II, when the highest number of immigrants came to the United States.

GO ON

12

> The Parties to this Treaty reaffirm their faith in the purposes and principles of the Charter of the United Nations and their desire to live in peace with all peoples and all governments.
>
> They are determined to safeguard the freedom, common heritage and civilisation [sic] of their peoples, founded on the principles of democracy, individual liberty and the rule of law.
>
> They seek to promote stability and well-being in the North Atlantic area.
>
> They are resolved to unite their efforts for collective defence [sic] and for the preservation of peace and security.
>
> —*The North Atlantic Treaty, April 4, 1949*

What is the significance of the North Atlantic Treaty?

A North Atlantic countries agreed to declare war on other countries when necessary.

B Nations that signed the treaty agreed to secure peace in the North Atlantic region.

C Countries found in the North Atlantic would be powerless to defend themselves.

D Governments rejected the treaty because the North Atlantic is a peaceful region.

13

Comparison of Political Systems

Canada	Cuba
Three branches of government	Three branches of government
Voting age: 18	Head of government: president
Head of state: Queen Elizabeth II	Unicameral legislature
Head of government: prime minister	Political party: Cuban Communist Party (PCC)
Bicameral parliament	Voting age: 16
Political parties: Bloc Québécois, Conservative Party of Canada, Green Party, Liberal Party, New Democratic Party	15 provinces

Which of the following statements is correct?

A Cuban voters have a choice of political parties, while Canadian voters are limited.

B While Canada is a representative government, Cuba appears to be a theocracy.

C While Canada is a monarchy, Cuba can be politically classified as a republic.

D Canada has ties to the British monarchy, while Cuba is a communist state.

14

Dubai	Saudi Arabia
Building Internet City—information center	Building dams—water for agricultural production

Which statement identifies the information shown in the chart?

A All countries in the Middle East are technologically advanced.

B Some countries use technology, while others prefer traditional ways.

C It is important for countries in Southwest Asia to keep up with technology.

D Technological innovations have been used to modify the physical environment.

15 In 1970, a powerful cyclone struck Bangladesh, a low-lying country located on a coastal plain in South Asia. Which statement best describes the impact of the cyclone?

A Local schools closed for a short time during clean-up operations.

B Nearby countries assisted in restoring power to isolated areas hit by rain.

C There was a significant loss of life and crops due to the intensity of the storm.

D Government assisted the people by providing temporary shelters in affected areas.

GO ON

16 Voting for the president of the United States occurs once every four years. Among the voters at a small town election center is an elderly woman who was born before the 1920 passage of the Nineteenth Amendment, granting women the right to vote. She tells the local election official that she has not missed voting in a presidential election since she turned 21 years old in 1939. How would the woman's voting habits be characterized?

A as an expression of nationalism

B as being similar to international women's rights

C as a public policy that can be changed at any time

D as part of a decision-making process affecting national policies

---

17 What has been the economic impact of overhead sprinkler systems on desert areas in the Negev Desert?

A the ability to mine precious gems

B an imposition of severe financial hardships

C a limited change to the way the land is used

D the conversion of desert area to agricultural zones

18

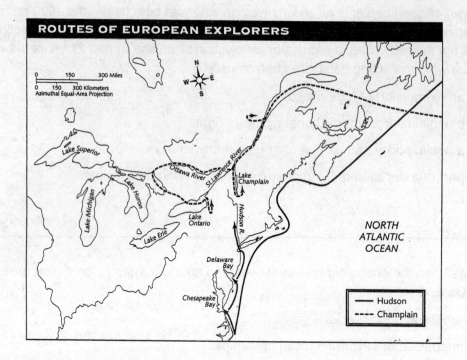

ROUTES OF EUROPEAN EXPLORERS

0   150   300 Miles
0   150   300 Kilometers
Azimuthal Equal-Area Projection

Lake Superior

Ottawa River

St. Lawrence River

Lake Champlain

Lake Michigan

Lake Huron

Lake Ontario

Lake Erie

Hudson R.

Delaware Bay

Chesapeake Bay

NORTH ATLANTIC OCEAN

——— Hudson
- - - - Champlain

Which statement does the map support?

A Early explorers competed for the most advantageous route.

B Hudson and Champlain influenced settlement of Lake Michigan.

C Water routes played a major role in the settlement of North America.

D Most settlement of North America occurred in an east-to-west pattern.

---

19 Though China has shown dramatic economic growth through globalization and diversification of its economy, much of the country remains a society dependent on a rural economy. Because of the distance from markets —

A Chinese farmers limit what they grow to conserve resources

B many of the Chinese depend on the government for food subsidies

C imported foodstuffs from other regions become staples for the Chinese

D the Chinese are self-sufficient in agriculture, especially in rice production

GO ON

68

20

Which statement is an accurate comparison of information shown on the map?

A Several new countries were created from Germany after World War II.

B The political borders of Germany remained intact after World War II.

C Germany experienced little political change following World War II.

D Germany came under foreign control following World War II.

---

21 During the late 19th-century industrialization in the United States, cities grew as factories increased in size and number. Factories advertised for workers. Young farmers left rural areas and headed to New York and Chicago in search of jobs and opportunities. Such migration is classified as —

A a push factor, caused by social issues

B a push factor, caused by natural disasters

C a pull factor, caused by political change

D a pull factor, caused by economics

22

> Though in the past, most Australians were of British descent, today high rates of immigration are changing the cultural characteristics of Australia. The people of Australia still share similar characteristics to the British, however, including driving on the left side of the road, the drinking of tea, and the practice of the Christian religion.

Which statement best describes the cultural characteristics of Australia?

A Australia is much different today than it was in the past.

B Australia is related to its social and cultural aspects.

C Religion is one part of the culture that has changed.

D Immigration continues to stabilize Australia.

23

> Tea is an important export for Sri Lanka. Tea plantations in Sri Lanka cover larger areas. Much like in the past, workers still fill baskets carried on their backs with tea leaves destined for foreign markets. Today, Sri Lanka is a leader in tea production. Other plantations in Sri Lanka produce rubber and coconuts, but tea remains Sri Lanka's prime agricultural commodity.

The description of tea plantations in Sri Lanka is an example of —

A diversification of crops in an effort to stabilize the economy

B the importance of foreign investment in developing countries

C the need for a large labor force to address manufacturing initiatives

D a culture that maintains traditional ways, including a traditional economy

24

As the American colonies were settled, regional economic, religious, and social characteristics developed based on immigration and physical features of the land. Large plantations were mostly found in —

A the Southern Colonies

B New England

C the Middle Colonies

D British Territory

25

Over the past fifty years, the Canadian economy has moved from one based on agriculture and manufacturing to one largely dependent on the service sector. Mining remains an important industry, as does fishing. Its three ocean coastlines—the Atlantic, the Pacific, and the Arctic—provide large fishing operations.

Large-scale fishing in Canada is considered —

A a cottage industry

B a commercial industry

C subsistence agriculture

D a service industry

26 Canadian geese return to a large public park in the Midwest each year. Their numbers are growing. The city council plans to discuss a public policy regarding the geese at its next public meeting. A group of citizens has already circulated a petition to give to the council, supporting a geese sanctuary at the park. What factors will influence the council's decision?

A Canadian geese are migratory birds that prefer to live near bodies of water.

B Canada is seeking ways to manage the population of the wild bird.

C Some like the geese at the park, while others find them to be a nuisance.

D Tourists traveling in Canada enjoy taking photographs of the geese.

27

The caste system in India has been a cornerstone of Hinduism for centuries. Four original castes—the Brahmins (priests and scholars), the Kshatriyas (rulers and warriors), the Vaisyas (farmers and merchants), and the Sudras (artisans and laborers)—over time were divided into smaller groups, including the untouchables, or lowest caste. According to Hindu belief, a person was born into a caste and remained so for life. Though the caste system is still practiced among Hindus today, it has come under scrutiny among those who value individual freedom and the principles of democracy.

Which phrase best describes the Hindu caste system?

A a part of the Hindu religion that is a relatively new practice

B a system that is at odds with individual freedoms and principles of democracy

C an idea that had its start when India broke its colonial ties with Europe

D an internationally accepted practice that has been adopted by other cultures

28 European colonization of Africa in the 19th century was driven by —

A the desire to exploit Africa's natural resources

B concern for the well-being of native animals

C migration southward due to ongoing wars

D the impact of African currency on Europe

29 What cultural change occurred in Somalia as a result of the combined difficulties of drought and warfare?

A differences in climate that affected the area

B disruption of traditional agricultural practices

C slight movement of the nation's northeastern border

D infusion of European currency into the local economy

73

30

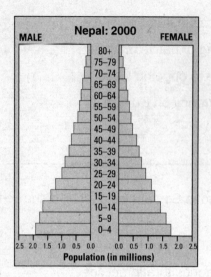

In analyzing the population pyramid of Nepal in 2000, it can be stated with relative certainty that in Nepal —

A the population was mostly elderly

B there was a high mortality rate among teenagers

C the life expectancy of people is relatively short

D most people lived productive and long lives

31

Mongolia	Taiwan
• Traditional ways have roots in ancient Chinese way of life • Shifting to a market economy • Gold, copper, and iron mining • Nomadic way of life still followed • Farms and ranches • Isolated from the west	• Population almost exclusively Chinese, well educated • Buddhism, Confucianism, Taoism • Mandarin mostly spoken • Electronics manufacturing • Rapid economic growth • Open to western influence

Which statement best summarizes the information in the bulleted lists?

A The cultures of Mongolia and Taiwan have roots in traditional Chinese ways.

B Mongolia and Taiwan are focused on building new industries.

C The people of Mongolia and Taiwan have similar economies.

D The people of Mongolia and Taiwan practice the same lifestyles.

74

32 The Trail of Tears defines the forced removal of the Cherokee from their native lands in Georgia to Indian Territory west of the Mississippi River. Which of the following is the most likely cultural impact on Native Americans forced to move from one area of the country to another very different area?

  A The Cherokee continued to farm and live as they had in Georgia.

  B Changes in climate and resources challenged ways of life in the Cherokee homeland.

  C All of the Cherokee culture remained with those who stayed in Georgia.

  D A blending of languages and religions resulted in new traditions and ways.

33 Which of the following statements is true about a global economy?

  A Powerful economies completely dominate the production of electronic goods.

  B Certain regions specialize in financially assisting others in the region.

  C Nations become dependent on each other for goods and services.

  D Every country in the world manufactures similar products.

34 Successive years of severe drought, crop diseases, and insect infestations that consume plants in agricultural regions result in —

  A political upheaval and civil war

  B famine and long-term shortages of food

  C environmental cooperation among countries

  D a redistribution of financial resources in the region

75

35 China has a population of approximately 1.34 billion. One out of every five people lives in China. In what way is China influencing international political relations in order to meet the needs of its growing population?

A by restricting its reliance on western medicine and returning to traditional ways

B by gaining control over neighboring lands to obtain needed natural resources

C by expanding its trade relations with other countries to grow economically

D by returning to the isolationist policies of the past to become self-sufficient

---

36 What occurs as storms move over coastal mountains?

A More precipitation is dropped on the windward side of the mountain.

B Inland regions receive more precipitation than coastal regions.

C Tornadoes have a tendency to stall as the storms move inland.

D Cyclones form as clouds move over the mountains inland.

37

WORLD POPULATIONS

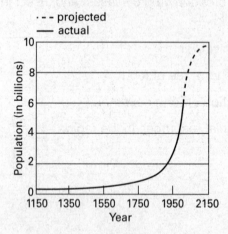

Which statement best describes the trend in world population growth shown by the graph?

A Population growth has stabilized over the past five centuries.

B Population dramatically increased in the 20th century.

C Population growth is dependent on health and technology.

D Population should decline worldwide in the next century.

38 Which occurs within the lithosphere?

    A earthquakes

    B cyclones

    C plant growth

    D tsunamis

---

39 The Dutch controlled the destructive power of the sea on coastlines by building structures called seaworks. These sea barriers include dikes to hold back the sea and high earthen platforms called terpen, which serve as places of safety during high tides or flooding. Such management of natural resources —

    A conflicts with current civil engineering principles addressing shoreline erosion

    B alters the planting and health of deciduous forests along the peninsula

    C affects the location and movement of people in the Netherlands

    D changes the migratory patterns of whales in the North Sea

---

40 How has the building of canals impacted Venice?

    A It has allowed a movement of goods between places.

    B It has caused severe loss of native habitat.

    C It has resulted in a reduction of tourist dollars.

    D It has brought about a change in sea level.

GO ON

41 Which of the following describes a situation that could benefit from use of the Global Positioning System (GPS)?

    A A local resident would like to view old roadways and bridges that still exist under a man-made lake.

    B A real estate broker wants a map of all waterfront parcels in the town to show to a prospective buyer.

    C An environmentalist needs to create a composite map of groundwater sources, roads, and forested areas.

    D A tour bus driver must make several stops along a route that is new to her. She has limited time to get from one place to another.

42 The tilt of the Earth is at a 23.5° angle in relation to the Sun. Because of this and the Earth's revolution around the Sun —

    A the seasons change

    B the tropic of Cancer moves

    C weather patterns remain constant

    D humidity is constant in the Northern Hemisphere

43

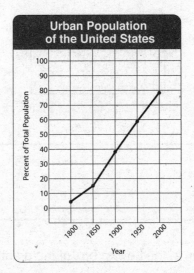

Urban Population of the United States

Which statement explains the relationship between past and present events shown by the graph?

A The United States moved from an agrarian to an industrialized society.

B Advances in science and technology assisted farmers in the United States.

C The United States expanded its foreign subsidies to aid rural development.

D People traveled in wagon trains and railroads to settle western United States.

44

In 1946, the country of Yugoslavia was divided into six republics: Bosnia and Herzegovina, Croatia, Macedonia, Montenegro, Serbia, and Slovenia. Two self-governing provinces, Kosovo and Vojvodina, made up Serbia. The division of land and people left Bosnia and Croatia ethnically mixed.

What resulted from the division of Yugoslavia into six republics?

A an eruption of political tensions and civil war

B a spirit of cooperation among all the six republics

C a unified military that controlled each country's borders

D an equal distribution of financial resources across the region

GO ON

45

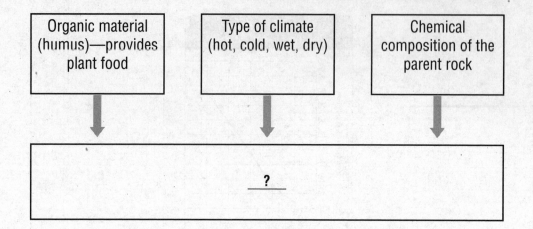

| Organic material (humus)—provides plant food | Type of climate (hot, cold, wet, dry) | Chemical composition of the parent rock |

?

Which phrase should be written in the bottom box of the graphic organizer?

A erosion

B weathering

C soil formation

D spatial diffusion

46

A young family sells its retail business in a small suburb and moves to a rural area. The family decides to raise goats and sell goat milk to the local cheese factory. The factory specializes in making goat cheese, exporting most of its product to European markets. Two members of the family start a construction business specializing in solar-heated barns, while a third teaches a business class at the local community college.

Which activity from the passage is considered a quaternary economic activity?

A teaching a college business class

B constructing solar-heated barns

C selling goat milk to markets overseas

D raising goats in order to sell goat milk

47 Which group contains areas classified as formal regions?

   A Southwest Asia, the Pacific Islands, Mississippi delta

   B Latin America, St. Lawrence Seaway, rain forests

   C the United States, France, the Nile River

   D East Asia, Europe, Africa

48 Which is an accurate statement about world population trends?

   A Rural populations are declining as megacities expand.

   B The rate of natural increase shows trends in infant mortality.

   C Population trends include live births, death rates, and crop distribution.

   D Japan leads the world in population growth, while Africa shows low birthrates.

49 Southwest Asia is an extremely arid region that receives less than 18 inches of precipitation each year. Much of the region is covered by sand, salt, or rocks. Vegetation is scarce except where areas have been irrigated and turned into productive farmland. What best describes another effect of irrigation?

   A urbanization

   B growth of settlements

   C expansion of the desert

   D increase of political freedoms

50 Which statement describes the free enterprise system?

A There is private ownership of businesses with the intent to make a profit.

B Government intervenes in allocating goods, resources, and prices.

C Government controls and distributes ownership of all business activity.

D Production of goods and services is determined by a central government.

51

What does the image depict?

A farming methods specific to one region

B ways of gathering water used by particular cultures

C a landscape representative of those in northern latitudes

D the importance of water to successful farming in dry areas

GO ON ➡

52 The use of mobile devices, such as smart phones and iPads, has gained in popularity worldwide. Many people use their mobile devices to connect to social media sites where they can communicate with others both nationally and internationally. What have mobile devices become?

A   an international language

B   a regional distinction

C   a cultural element

D   a political unit

53

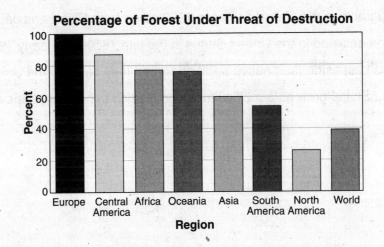

Percentage of Forest Under Threat of Destruction

Which statement explains the information shown on the graph?

A   Many countries are trying to preserve natural resources.

B   Urbanization and changes in land use are occurring worldwide.

C   Several countries are establishing nature preserves.

D   People worldwide are addressing global warming.

> "Give me your tired, your poor,
>
> Your huddled masses yearning to breathe free,
>
> The wretched refuse of your teeming shore.
>
> Send these, the homeless, tempest-tost to me,
>
> I lift my lamp beside the golden door!"
>
> —From "The New Colossus," by Emma Lazarus,
> 1883, mounted inside the pedestal of the
> Statue of Liberty in 1903

Which statement best describes the outcome of the sentiments expressed in the poem?

A Most immigrants to the United States in 1883 came from China and Japan.

B Immigration declined in the United States in the late 1800s and early 1900s.

C Immigrants cast aside their native traditions when they came to the United States.

D The United States grew as a multicultural society rich in new traditions and languages.

55

Causes of Wetland Loss :
1986 to 1997

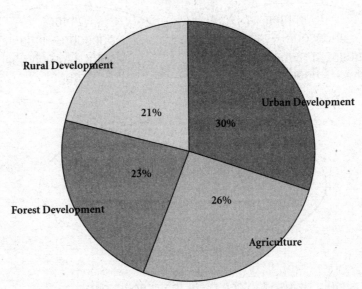

Rural Development 21%

Urban Development 30%

Forest Development 23%

26%

Agriculture

What conclusion can you draw from the information shown in the graph?

A Loss of wetlands to urban development serves the needs of growing communities.

B Many environmentalists oppose policies that allowed for the loss of wetlands.

C Conversion of land from one use to another has little environmental impact.

D Policies regarding wetlands allow for a conversion of land use.

---

56 Many of Mexico's factories are found near the border it shares with the United States. Manufacturing is a significant part of Mexico's growing economy. What is the most likely advantage of locating manufacturing centers near the Mexico-United States border?

A young labor force in need of employment

B availability of land for construction of factories

C ease of exportation to markets in the United States

D proximity to the Rio Grande as a water source

South Asia Monsoon Seasons

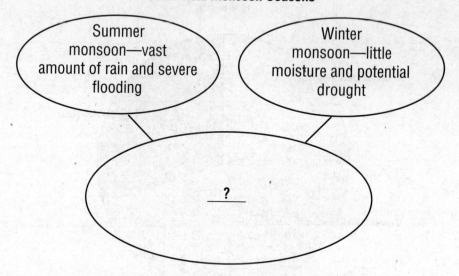

Which statement should be used to complete the graphic organizer?

A Summer monsoons are important to the agricultural economy of India.

B A balance of wet and dry seasons is critical for agriculture in the region.

C People throughout region grow different crops to adapt to winter monsoons.

D Modifying how people grow crops can help to increase agricultural production.

---

58 The formation of the Himalayas was caused by —

A the collision of two continental plates along a convergent boundary

B movement of two continental plates along a divergent boundary

C the spreading of tectonic plates along a divergent boundary

D the sliding of continental plates along a transform boundary

GO ON ➡

Name _____ Date _____

59

In 1967, Israel took control of the city of Jerusalem as part of the Six-Day War. Israel also gained control of the West Bank and the Gaza Strip. Following its capture, the city of Jerusalem expanded. Palestinian Arabs opposed the expansion of Jerusalem.

In 1993, the Oslo Accords allowed for Palestinian self-rule in the West Bank and the Gaza Strip. Ongoing conflict over the right by Arabs to establish a Palestinian state continues to destabilize the region politically.

Which phrase describes the dynamics of the region from 1967 to present?

A unified peace effort

B international weakness

C political and human turmoil

D foreign and domestic stability

60 Every winter, artists in Jukkasjärvi, Sweden, create an ice hotel out of 10,000 tons of ice and 30,000 tons of snow. People from around the world pay to stay at the ice hotel. This is an example of —

A the creativity of individuals living in mild climates

B how individuals adapt to variations in hours of daylight

C the importance of tourism to temperate climate countries

D how changes in climate affect patterns of economic activity

61

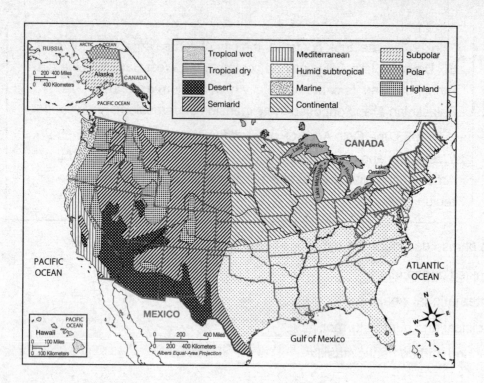

What is used to categorize regions in this map?

A climate

B political units

C river systems

D latitude

---

62 The United States established the Department of Homeland Security and supported the efforts of the president to form an international coalition in direct response to —

A aggressive attacks by Albanian guerrillas in Kosovo

B the breaking away of the Soviet republics in the early 1990s

C the threat of a nuclear weapons program undertaken by Iran

D terrorist attacks on September 11, 2001, by al-Qaeda operatives

GO ON

63 The federal government encouraged western movement of settlers to the central and western regions of the United States during the second half of the 19th century, displacing Native Americans. Railroads brought people to the West. Railroads also transported western cattle and products to markets in the East. Eventually, the frontier was settled. What is this an example of?

A economic and governmental relationship with settlements and the environment

B sustainable development of resources that previously had little value

C undue hardship placed on those who sought to settle in the Midwest

D management of non-renewable resources by a federal agency

---

64 Which of the following shows the correct cause-and-effect relationship?

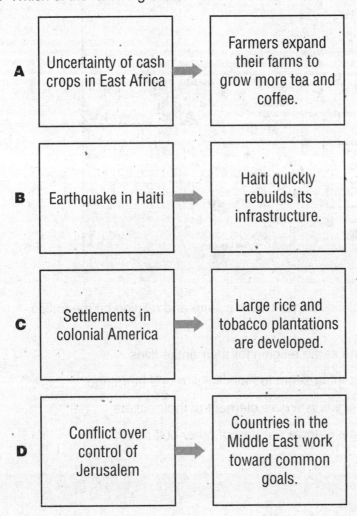

A Uncertainty of cash crops in East Africa → Farmers expand their farms to grow more tea and coffee.

B Earthquake in Haiti → Haiti quickly rebuilds its infrastructure.

C Settlements in colonial America → Large rice and tobacco plantations are developed.

D Conflict over control of Jerusalem → Countries in the Middle East work toward common goals.

GO ON

65 Which is an accurate statement on the changing role of women in North Africa?

A Women maintain traditional roles in many households.

B Women earn equal pay for equal work in Tunisia.

C Women cover their faces with scarves in Egypt.

D Women eat and pray separately from men.

66

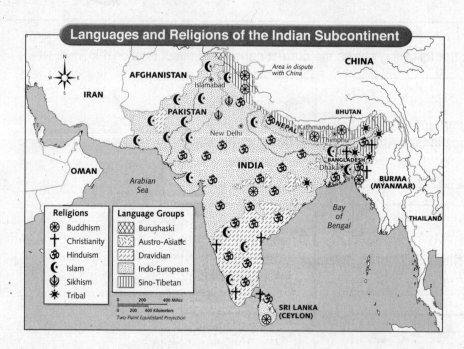

According to the map, what is the relationship between culture and religion on the Indian subcontinent?

A Most people in India practice the same religion for their entire lives.

B The major religions practiced in India seem to have links to one language.

C For many in India, the Hindu religion is a core element of their culture.

D Religions practiced by the people of India are part of other cultures.

67 In 1994, Rwanda was in the midst of a civil war. During that year, over one million Rwandans migrated to other countries in Africa. Such migration is classified as —

    A a push factor, caused by environmental issues

    B a push factor, caused by political upheaval

    C a pull factor, caused by social concerns

    D a pull factor, caused by economics

---

68 The landscape of Texas is a combination of urban life and the wide open spaces that support an abundance of wildlife. One thing that is unique about Texas is that there are —

    A mountain areas found in every region of the state from east to west

    B large tracts of prairie grasslands in the extreme western region of the state

    C similarities of tree species from the northern to southern sections of the state

    D varied lands, from coastal plains that receive large amounts of rain to desert valleys

Practice Test 2

1

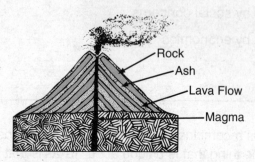

Stratovolcano

Rock
Ash
Lava Flow
Magma

What is the effect of the physical process shown in the diagram?

A rapid climate change

B creation of a new landform

C formation of a tectonic plate

D erosion of a large rock

2 Which statement describes what occurred as railroad tracks were laid from east to west across the United States during the late 1800s?

A Cattle ranching declined as people moved west to start small farms.

B Growth of the transportation industry slowed the growth of factories.

C Towns grew and businesses started to meet the needs of settlers.

D Government sought to regulate and set limits on business profits.

3

World Continents

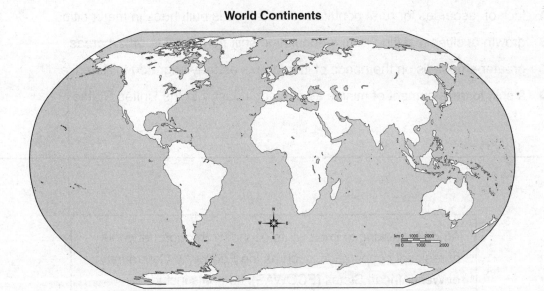

Which group of factors influences the distribution of climate regions across the continents?

A elevation, latitude, wind systems, mountain barriers

B landforms, revolution of the Earth, volcanic eruptions, elevation

C the equator, latitude, tectonic forces, wind systems

D soil-building processes, wind systems, latitude, temperature

---

4 Bagpipes are played in Scotland. Drums are a popular percussion instrument in Africa. Both bagpipes and drums represent —

A traditions that remain localized due to their religious nature

B examples of folk music that are quite popular throughout the world

C similar melodies that characterize music found in both hemispheres

D elements of culture that make specific regions of the world distinctive

5 One impact of industrialization occurring in the United States during the late 19th century was —

A lack of resources for rural populations as railroads built hubs in major cities

B growth of cities resulting from a population shift from rural to urban areas

C greater emphasis on the needs of immigrants as they migrated to America

D a shift to development of mining as a major industry in the United States

6

> Africa is seeking to improve its economy through networks of regional cooperation, such as the Economic Community of West African States (ECOWAS). Its goals include improving transportation and promoting trade.

Which of the following will help Africa grow its economy and best satisfy basic needs?

A returning to subsistence farming

B focusing on one commodity for export

C expanding commercial agriculture production

D reducing foreign investment in commercial industries

7 Many places in the United States are known for their regional identity. Examples of such cultural elements include universities, historical sites, and language. Which of the following best describes another element of culture?

A a restaurant in Washington, D.C., highlighting cheese from Wisconsin on its menu

B a shop along the interstate selling souvenirs that are made in China

C an Internet site for guitarists that promotes metal guitar strings as superior to nylon

D a group of high school students attending class on Monday in October

8

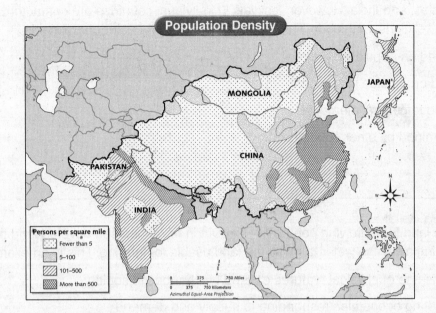

According to the population density map, which of the following statements is true?

A Most settlements occur inland where farmland is plentiful.

B High population areas are found along coastal regions.

C Population is evenly distributed across water routes.

D Settlements are influenced by industrial zones.

9 Which statement can be made about the summer solstice?

A Direct rays from the Sun occur near the tropic of Capricorn.

B It occurs as approximately the same time as the vernal equinox.

C It occurs yearly and is an indication of seasonal change.

D The days are equal in length across the entire world.

10 Religious festivals are celebrated in several countries, including Mexico, Brazil, Hong Kong, the United States, and India. However, festivals in individual countries are characterized by different costumes, religions, and foods. This highlights that the character of a place is —

   A focused on populated areas

   B based on outside influences

   C related to cultural elements

   D determined by other countries

---

11 To provide land for a growing population, the Dutch reclaimed sea-covered land by building dikes and pumping away the water to make the land usable for farming. This is an example of —

   A diverse use of physical features caused by changes in society

   B competing economies responding to supply and demand

   C the need for new laws restricting changes in land use

   D protecting limited natural resources of a region

---

12 The human development index considers education, health, and income when comparing the standard of living found in different countries. In contrast, another indicator, the gross domestic product, uses —

   A a calculation of standard of living based on which country is more developed

   B the number of newly industrialized areas found in a country

   C the monetary value of all finished goods and services

   D a comparison of wealth among population groups

GO ON

13

Characteristics of Three Political Systems

United States	United Kingdom	Iran
• Power balanced among three branches of federal government • Free elections • Power distributed between the federal, state, and local governments • Constitutional rights • Specific powers granted to the states	• Head of state: Queen Elizabeth II • Legislative body: Parliament • Voting rights • Political parties • Individual rights guaranteed	• Elections held • Supreme Leader appoints the judiciary • Highest state authority: president of Iran • Government leaders must maintain allegiance to the Islamic revolution • President carries out government decisions • President answers to Supreme Leader

Which of the following statements is correct?

A The United Kingdom is a totalitarian government.

B The government of Iran is classified as a theocracy.

C Both the United States and Iran hold free elections.

D All power is held at the federal level in the United States.

14

EUROPE AFTER THE COLD WAR

LEGEND

Formerly a communist country or region

Formerly a republic of the Soviet Union

Formerly East Germany

Based on the map, what significant political change occurred as a result of the Cold War?

A the spread of democracy to former communist states

B a military alliance between the former Soviet republics

C a series of treaties that ensured peace across the region

D the redrawing of political boundaries to pre-World War II boundaries

15 Canada, the United States, and Mexico signed the North American Free Trade Agreement (NAFTA) in 1994 to improve the economic health of the three countries and promote —

A air quality through new environmental standards

B cooperative international political relations

C an international student exchange program

D protection of endangered species

GO ON

16

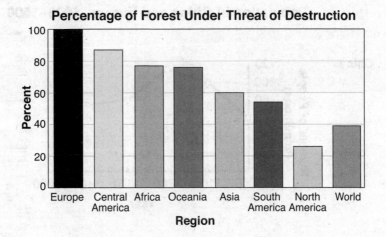

Percentage of Forest Under Threat of Destruction

What can you infer from the information shown on the graph?

A Governments value development more than protecting the region's natural resources.

B Governments establish uniform policies worldwide to protect natural resources.

C Government works with businesses to ensure limited use of natural resources.

D Government policies prevent regional overuse of vital natural resources.

17 On April 28, 1986, one of the nuclear reactors at a Soviet nuclear power plant in the city of Chernobyl exploded. Which statement describes the impact of that explosion?

A Radiation was limited to a small area, but the region remains closed today.

B Today, the area where the explosion took place is a thriving agricultural region.

C It is difficult to tell what the long-term regional effects will be on the population.

D A radioactive cloud quickly dissipated, minimizing the regional effects of the event.

GO ON

18

Population in China and Europe, 1000–1500

China

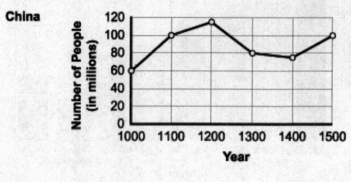

Europe

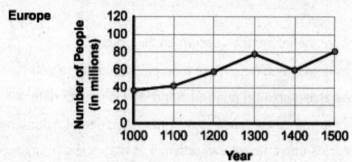

Which statement best describes the trend in world population growth shown by the graphs?

A The population of China and Europe declined from 1200 to 1400.

B Population in China and Europe rose between 1100 and 1400.

C Both China and Europe showed steady growth in population.

D Population in China and Europe rebounded after 1400.

GO ON

19

> Bullet trains, popular in Europe and in Japan, are being planned for the United States. Bullet trains move passengers at high speeds. As people choose to travel via bullet train, the number of gas-powered vehicles on roads will decrease. Wind turbines can be built along the bullet train corridor, allowing for two productive land uses.

What is one advantage of bullet trains?

A They require significant amounts of land developed for train stations to accommodate riders.

B They add significant costs for the public because of the need to generate construction funds.

C They address both future transportation needs and environmental concerns in positive ways.

D They should be very popular among people of the United States, who will utilize them on a daily basis.

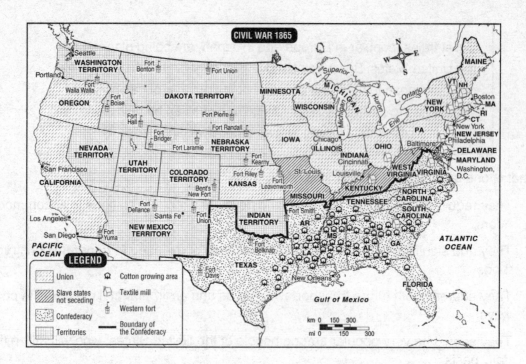

According to information on the map, what best characterizes the country in 1865?

A a Southern rural economy based on a slave labor system versus a Northern urban economy based on a manufacturing system

B expansion of the South that included the territories in the North and an interest in equal rights and freedom for every citizen

C traditions fostered by a shared history of farming and plantation life and the desire to settle the country in the West

D a unified government based on shared principles of liberty and a growing economy based on cotton and textiles

GO ON

21

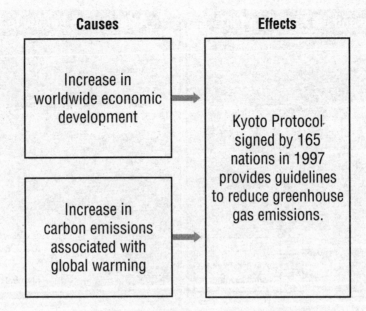

Causes   Effects

Increase in worldwide economic development

Increase in carbon emissions associated with global warming

Kyoto Protocol signed by 165 nations in 1997 provides guidelines to reduce greenhouse gas emissions.

Which statement best explains the information shown on the chart?

A Globalization requires that nations improve technology-based economies.

B Little has occurred in the past decade to improve the environment.

C Countries across the globe have industrialized their economies.

D Humans depend on and modify the physical environment.

GO ON

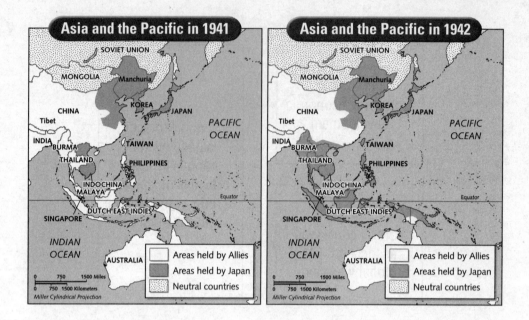

Which statement about political power in 1941 and 1942 is supported by the maps?

A   The areas controlled by Japan diminished after 1941.

B   There were more neutral countries in 1942 than in 1941.

C   The Allies lost control of most of the Dutch East Indies by 1942.

D   The political boundaries of China changed between 1941 and 1942.

---

23 The Ganges is a river that begins in a Himalayan glacier and flows to the Bay of Bengal. Of what importance is the Ganges to the region?

A   It was the first river settled in northern Asia.

B   Human life in the region strongly depends on it.

C   It is honored by many for its important military history.

D   It was the first river affected by laws prohibiting settlement.

GO ON ➡

Name _____ Date _____

24 Mexico suffers from high unemployment, increased violence due to trafficking of illegal drugs, and a decrease in foreign investments in Mexican businesses. Many Mexicans immigrate to the United States in search of work. Leaving Mexico to find a job in the United States is considered to be —

A a pull factor, prompted by social concerns

B a push factor, prompted by environmental issues

C a push factor, prompted by political division

D a pull factor, prompted by economics

25

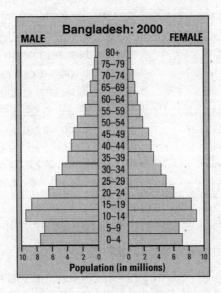

Based on the information shown in this population pyramid, the population of Bangladesh in 2000 —

A had an uneven standard of living among young and old

B grew at an even rate among males and females in all age ranges

C experienced greater infant mortality rates among males than females

D required a government investment in youth services and educational facilities

26 A development company is looking to build houses and an industrial park in the last remnant of an established wetland. A previous development there appears to have been successful. A local environmental group opposes the idea. What is one way the environmental group could express its opposition?

A pass an ordinance that prohibits any further building in wetlands

B provide a history of denial by the county zoning office to build in wetlands

C present a petition to the governor, signed by a majority of people in the area

D make a list of native plants and animals and present it to the state legislature

---

27

Rain Forest	Australian Desert
• Hot and humid • Biodiversity • Farming • Sale of timber • Livestock grazing • Deforestation due to farming and development • Highly populated	• Hot and dry • Crops requiring irrigation • Sparsely populated • Raising of some livestock • Little vegetation • Colonized by Europeans • Limited biodiversity

Which statement summarizes the information shown in the chart?

A Changes in climate and resources affect the location of economic activity.

B Population changes are affected by how people manage natural resources.

C Humans make good use of regional resources to build shelters and grow food.

D Changes in the environment caused by natural disasters force humans to adapt.

GO ON

28 Why did Germany invade Austria in 1938 and Poland in 1939?

   A It was a way to finally put an end to World War II.

   B It was an effort to assist countries suffering from war.

   C It was a means of controlling the resources and people in Austria and Poland.

   D It was an insistence by the European Union to take control.

29 During the 1930s, the Great Plains suffered extensive drought conditions. Combined with poor farming methods, the results were mile-high dust storms that devastated the area. Many fled to California in search of jobs and a new life. This type of migration is classified as a —

   A pull factor, prompted by economics

   B pull factor, prompted by social issues

   C push factor, prompted by political upheaval

   D push factor, prompted by environmental difficulties

30 The United States economy has strong manufacturing and agriculture sectors, and it is based on free enterprise. In this economic system —

   A everyone shares equally in profits generated

   B the government controls production and sales

   C private individuals own resources and profits

   D no regulations are placed on production or sales

GO ON

31 The nuclear explosion at Chernobyl is an example of why it is important to —

  A ignore the impact of technology on natural resources

  B continually monitor advanced technology

  C maintain secure and secret records on environmental impacts

  D limit tracking of radiation to specific countries

32

Which of the following is highlighted in this drawing?

  A cultural elements

  B religious character

  C the importance of language

  D the value of a good education

33 By removing salt from ocean water, desalinization —

    A assists with new water projects in the upper Midwest

    B encourages wasteful use of water in regions that are water starved

    C supplies water for wastewater treatment plants in Southwest Asia

    D further pollutes the environment in regions of France and Great Britain

34 The Sultan Ahmed Cami Mosque located in Turkey and a Buddhist temple located in Chufu, China, are examples of distinct —

    A building techniques based on available resources

    B religious architecture as a cultural element

    C buildings that have stood the test of time

    D religious tolerance

35 The Inca living in Peru in the 1200s carved terraces on steep mountains, planted crops, and developed irrigation systems to water the crops. In this way, they turned barren land into —

    A sustainable development using renewable resources

    B a much larger area for expansion of the Inca settlement

    C a non-renewable resource that requires human intervention

    D an area that could be used to protect the settlement against invaders

Climograph

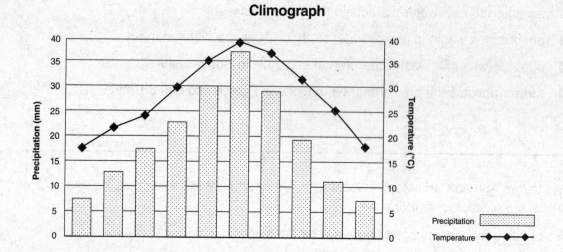

According to the information shown on the climograph, which biome is being identified?

A tropical rain forest

B deciduous and mixed forest

C desert and dry shrub

D tropical grassland

37 Which of the following is an example of cultural change brought about by diffusion?

A resistance to improving the social status of women in China

B trade agreements between the United States and Canada

C the number of individuals speaking Spanglish

D identification of ethnic groups in Africa

GO ON

38

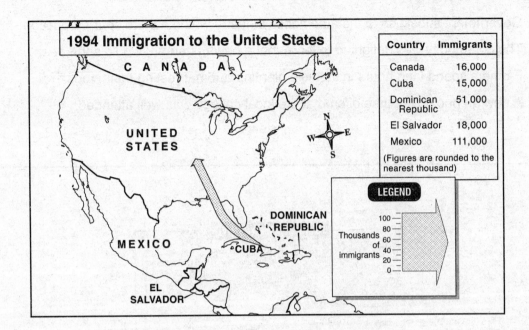

1994 Immigration to the United States

Country	Immigrants
Canada	16,000
Cuba	15,000
Dominican Republic	51,000
El Salvador	18,000
Mexico	111,000

(Figures are rounded to the nearest thousand)

LEGEND

Thousands of immigrants
100
80
60
40
20
0

Using the map, what can you infer about the impact of immigration in 1994?

A Most immigrants settled in the South and Midwest.

B French became the prominent language in the Northeast.

C The United States was enriched by Spanish foods and music.

D Trade among nations in the Northern Hemisphere decreased.

39 Sandstorms, like the one that struck Jingchang, China, can cause millions of dollars in damage and kill hundreds of people. Sandstorms are an example of —

A a disaster that is limited to certain parts of Asia

B a common event experienced by many parts of Europe

C a rare natural resource found in limited parts of the world

D a natural event that can have significant consequences for humans

GO ON ➡

40 Which of the following is a statement about tertiary economic activities?

A Government subsidies to the automobile industry was meant to spur production.

B The community was delighted to learn that a new restaurant would soon open.

C Farmers spend long hours in the field planting and harvesting their crops.

D A new archeology course offered at the local college was well attended.

41

How are regions defined on the map?

A by agricultural zones

B by political units

C by waterways

D by climate

42 Texas has a rich and varied culture built on its history and highlighted by its spirit of independence. Many people in Texas take pride in their Spanish heritage, expressed by —

A language, religion, and music

B work to sustain native plants

C laws that limit immigration

D architecture, pets, and clothing

43

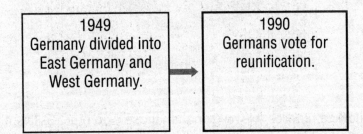

| 1949 Germany divided into East Germany and West Germany. | → | 1990 Germans vote for reunification. |

What was the result of the events shown in the graphic organizer?

A Germany remained a divided country with two separate governments.

B Germany restructured its political borders to become three republics.

C The Soviet Union annexed Germany and enlarged its political region.

D The political border between East Germany and West Germany dissolved.

GO ON ➡

44

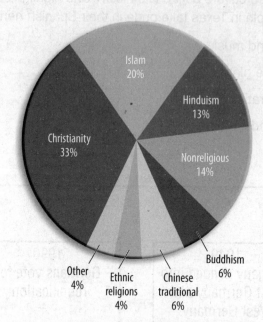

Fewer people worldwide practice this religion than those who practice Islam. Its founder Siddhartha Gautama, rejected Hinduism, and instead spent his life encouraging individuals to seek enlightenment. This religion is practiced by people living in China and Southeast Asia.

Which religion is described by the graph and narrative?

A Islam

B Christianity

C Chinese traditional

D Buddhism

45 East Asia has become a manufacturing center for clothing and electronics. Products are exported from East Asia to countries worldwide, which subsequently builds the economies of East Asian countries. This exchange of goods and building of regional economies is an example of —

A globalization

B political will

C local investment

D environmental impact

GO ON

46 Which is an example of a cottage industry?

A large automobile manufacturing plant

B sale of woodcrafts from a home workshop

C restaurant chain specializing in family-style service

D dairy farm selling milk to the local cheese factory

---

47 Which statement correctly describes chemical weathering?

A Material is moved by wind, water, ice, or gravity.

B Minerals break down when combined with air or water.

C Pieces of the Earth's lithosphere move from place to place.

D Large rock breaks into smaller rock of the same composition.

---

48 One result of the Columbian Exchange was the —

A transfer of agricultural plants from the Americas to Europe

B decrease in cultural diffusion from one region to another

C growth of the Native American population along coastal areas

D establishment of a representative government for the colonies

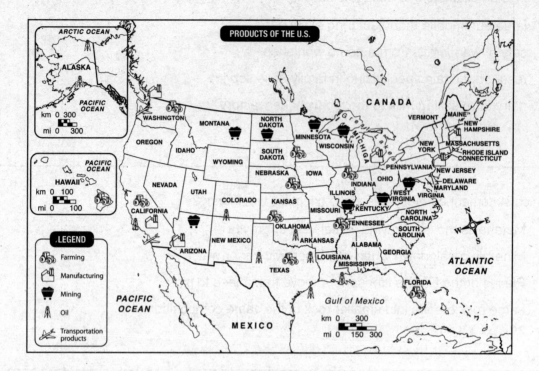

Based on information shown on the map, technology has —

A contributed only to the development of the upper Midwest

B been used in limited ways in agriculture in the past two centuries

C taken precedence over communication inventions since the early 1900s

D had significant impacts on agriculture and the exploitation of natural resources

---

50 The once-thriving Aral Sea in Central Asia has been negatively affected by the diversion of river water flowing into the Aral Sea to irrigation projects, as well as by agricultural processes that polluted the water and killed marine life. One result has been —

A improved health among the people of Central Asia

B a significant population shift away from the region

C investment of foreign capital to grow area businesses

D officials reversing construction of a large irrigation canal

51 Ocean currents move globally in large, circular systems. They affect the temperature of a region and —

A continental drift occurring over a span of time

B the amount of precipitation a region receives

C earthquake activity occurring in a region

D the seasons near the lower latitudes

---

52 Rift valleys form when —

A volcanoes erupt over a period of several years

B lake beds dry up after successive years of drought

C continental plates pull apart over millions of years

D precipitation falls during the annual monsoon season

53

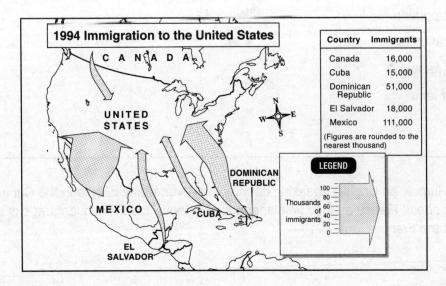

Which of the following is supported by information on the map?

A Most of the people living in the Dominican Republic immigrated to the United States.

B Jobs were created in the United States as a result of immigration trends in the 1990s.

C Emigration from the United States in 1994 equaled immigration to the United States.

D Spanish-speaking immigrants outnumbered French- and English-speaking immigrants.

54

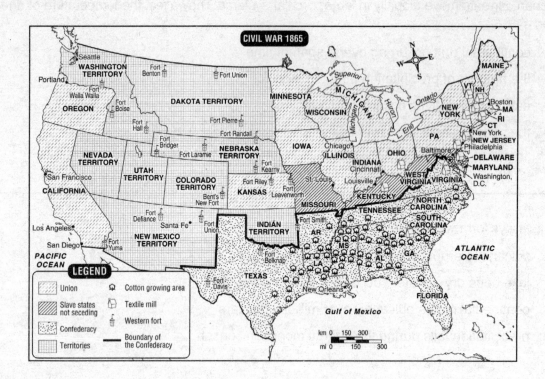

Based on information shown in the map, which of the following cultural patterns made the Confederacy a distinct region in 1865?

A public opinion

B political units

C water routes

D use of land

---

55 Canada is largely an English-speaking country. However, many people in the Canadian province of Quebec speak French as their first language. For them, the French language is an essential element of the French-Canadian —

A religion

B culture

C education

D economics

56 In 2010, a catastrophic earthquake struck Haiti, an economically depressed country. More than 200,000 people died. Which of the following best describes other consequences of the earthquake on the people of Haiti?

   A tornadoes that devastated hotels along the coastline

   B lack of international support in providing medical aid

   C a breakdown in the transportation and communication systems

   D a secondary tsunami that caused more damage than the earthquake

---

57

> **We the Peoples of the United Nations Determined**
>
> • to save succeeding generations from the scourge of war, which twice in our lifetime has brought untold sorrow to mankind, and
>
> • to reaffirm faith in fundamental human rights, in the dignity and worth of the human person, in the equal rights of men and women and of nations large and small, and
>
> • to establish conditions under which justice and respect for the obligations arising from treaties and other sources of international law can be maintained, and
>
> • to promote social progress and better standards of life in larger freedom...
>
>   *—Preamble to the United Nations Charter, June 26, 1945*

What is the purpose of the United Nations?

   A to work cooperatively for international peace and security

   B to take over control of a government when it threatens war

   C to promote worldwide goals, such as a single international language

   D to establish a military presence in countries that violate international law

GO ON

Which statement about the hydrosphere is supported by the information on the map?

A Winds blowing over ocean currents affect climate.

B The Gulf Stream moderates the temperature of Europe.

C Ocean currents move warm water away from the equator.

D Ocean currents affect the amount of precipitation an area receives.

---

59 The Silk Road spanned 4,000 miles across what is today Kazakhstan, Kyrgyzstan, Tajikistan, Turkmenistan, and Uzbekistan. The Silk Road is an example of a region defined by —

A a trade network

B political units

C language

D religion

60

> Aboriginal people of Australia lived by hunting and gathering. They considered the land sacred. Because the Aboriginal people did not farm, mine, or build on the land, the British felt they had no ties to the land. The British government declared the land to be *Terra Nullius,* or empty land.
>
> British settlers began settling Australia in 1788. They chose the most fertile land for settlement. The British government forced the Aboriginal people to live in parts of Australia where the land was less productive.

Which of the following best describes what occurred in Australia in 1788?

A Farmers always prefer the most fertile ground.

B Changes in society can lead to diverse use of the land.

C Common land use was practiced by different cultures.

D It is important to make the most productive use of land.

---

61 In 1994, over one million Rwandans left Rwanda due to —

A an attempt to wipe out the Kurds in Iraq

B conflict and destruction as a result of the civil war

C religious strife between Muslims and non-Muslims

D famine striking the country of Somalia in East Africa

---

62 An example of a functional region would be —

A the Midwest

B the United States

C prairies of the Great Plains

D the New York City subway system

The Muslim Influence on Trade

Region	Exports to Muslim Traders	Imports from Muslim Traders
Soninkes in West Africa	gold	salt
Ghana, Kanem, and Gao	gold, ivory, cotton cloth, and slaves	salt, horses, weapons, glass, and jewels
Mali	gold, grain, and cotton	salt, silk, ceramics, and jewels
Songhay	gold, ebony, ivory, slaves, and cotton	salt, beads, ceramics, and silk
Swahili City-States	gold, salt, and ivory	ceramics and jewelry
India	precious stones, perfumes, aloes, teakwood, salt, coconuts, slaves, and spices	horses, cloth, and slaves
China	silk, porcelain, and spices	dates, sugar, cloth, perfumes, and precious stones

What conclusion can you draw based on the information in the table?

A Throughout time, trade has been vibrant and localized.

B As time progressed, trade expanded to North America.

C During ancient times, trade was restricted to Asia.

D Even in the past, trade was global in nature.

64

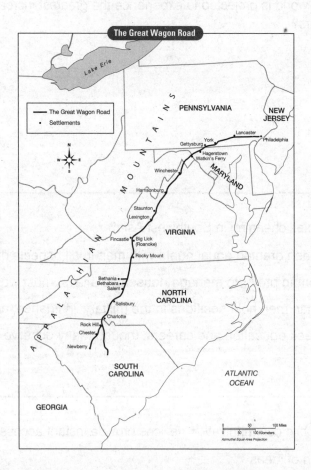

What can you conclude from information shown on the map?

A Settlement occurred from the northwest to the southeast.

B New settlements occurred along the established route.

C Most people settled near an abundant water source.

D Regional differences occurred along wagon routes.

65 The Canadian national anthem is played before the start of a professional hockey game held in Canada. The playing of the national anthem is an expression of —

A diverse cultures

B public policy

C nationalism

D patriotism

66 Which region of the world is projected to experience the greatest increase in population in the next twenty-five years?

   A Asia

   B Africa

   C Europe

   D South America

---

67 How are women's roles changing in Southwest Asia?

   A Women have been granted equal rights with men in all aspects of society.

   B While some women prefer to manage household affairs, most work in government.

   C More women than men hold positions in the military, in finance, and in leadership.

   D More women seek education and careers, though many observe traditional lifestyles.

---

68 The Internet and mobile communication devices provide instant access to information and —

   A the globalization of ideas

   B restrictions on social networking

   C a return to the traditions of the past

   D a reduction in light pollution in urban areas